He leaned forward and kissed her.

Amber stood stock-still in shock. His lips were warm and firm, moving against hers in invitation. He didn't touch her anywhere except on the mouth, which was more than enough. She felt light-headed. Slowly she leaned into the kiss, savoring the sensations that spread through her like melted butter. He made no further demands, didn't push for more, just let his lips caress hers while she thought she would float away in delight.

Her heart was pounding when he ended the kiss. He stayed close, his breath soughing across her cheeks. Slowly, Amber opened her eyes.

"You can't kiss me," she said, trying to sound forceful. That wispy voice couldn't be hers. "I'm a widow."

Babies on the Way

*Mother & daughter find themselves
unexpectedly pregnant—at the same time!*

Meet Sara Simpson in
THEIR PREGNANCY BOMBSHELL

At 38, she's finally got an empty nest and is celebrating
the start of her new life.... She's decided that now is the
time to start again, have some fun and travel
the world...and she meets the man who is happy
to do the same. Then Sara discovers she's
fallen pregnant on their wedding night....

Meet her daughter in
PREGNANT: FATHER NEEDED

Widow Amber Woodworth is making a new life for
herself as an independent, single mum-to-be. Her
new neighbor, Adam Carruthers, is a sexy fireman...
but Amber's determined not to get involved again,
especially to a man who, like her late husband,
puts his life on the line—every day....

THEIR PREGNANCY BOMBSHELL (#3847)
*was on sale June 2005 in Harlequin Romance®
Available at www.eHarlequin.com—while stock lasts!*

PREGNANT: FATHER NEEDED

Barbara McMahon

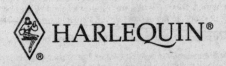

TORONTO • NEW YORK • LONDON
AMSTERDAM • PARIS • SYDNEY • HAMBURG
STOCKHOLM • ATHENS • TOKYO • MILAN • MADRID
PRAGUE • WARSAW • BUDAPEST • AUCKLAND

FDNY—We'll Always Remember
To the men and women
of the United States Armed Forces—Thank you.
May you all return home to live long and prosper.

ISBN 0-373-03851-8

PREGNANT: FATHER NEEDED

First North American Publication 2005.

Copyright © 2005 by Barbara McMahon.

www.eHarlequin.com

Printed in U.S.A.

PROLOGUE

AMBER WOODWORTH sat in the front of the small church, trying her best to ignore the words the minister spoke. Her gaze was fixed on the flag-draped coffin at the front. Her husband of less than three months was inside. She still couldn't believe it. How could Jimmy have been talking on the phone with her one day and dead three days later? Their marriage hadn't really started. Now it would never unfold as they once dreamed.

Tears threatened again. She took a deep breath. If she could just hold on a little longer, she could escape to the sanctuary of her apartment and fall into tiny pieces.

Her mother reached out and squeezed her hand. Amber tried to smile at her, but it was too hard. Her mother and new stepfather, Matt, had been so supportive these last few days. Amber didn't know what she would have done without them. She knew she could depend on them to help her in every way possible. But it would never change the fact she had to go on alone.

No, not quite alone.

She hugged her secret. Her mother knew, and Matt. But no one else. She hadn't even had a chance to tell Jimmy.

Now he would never know he would have become a father in November.

She glanced at her mother. She was also pregnant—with Matt's child. How odd to be pregnant the same time as her mother. Her friend Kathy from high school was pregnant, but that was normal. Not that her mother was so old, but Amber still felt it peculiar to know she and her mother would have their babies practically at the same time. Would she ever think of that child as a brother or sister? She'd literally be old enough to be its mother.

The minister finished his eulogy and the last hymn was sung. On her left, Jimmy's mother sobbed. Amber knew Virginia Woodworth would grieve her son's passing the rest of her life. She had doted on him. Maybe too much.

Amber remembered how uncomfortable she'd been with Virginia interfering in their brief marriage. The woman had stopped by the apartment almost every day. Amber sometimes thought Jimmy stayed at the Army Base to avoid his mother.

That was unkind. He had been involved in his job. But she'd resented the time he'd spent at work or staying overnight at the Base when he could have been with her. If they'd known he had such a short time remaining, would it have made a difference?

The trip to the cemetery passed in a blur. As did the short graveside service. When Taps sounded, Amber let the tears fall. She would never see Jimmy again. Never laugh with him, or plan a wonderful future together. She'd loved him since age fifteen. Almost five years. She had always thought they'd spend the rest of their lives together.

The military honor guard folded the flag, and handed it to the lieutenant. He stepped to her and offered it.

"On behalf of a grateful nation," he said solemnly.

She took it, hugging it to her breasts, looking through her tears at the polished casket. She would be twenty next month, and she was already a widow. How could she go on without the man she'd planned to spend her life with?

"It should have been mine," Virginia wailed. "He was my son for longer than he was her husband. It should have come to me."

Her husband tried to hush her, drawing her into his arms, but her cries grew louder. The others stared at her.

Amber was startled. She looked at her mother.

"Do I give it to her?" Amber asked.

Sara shook her head and spoke softly for only Amber. "It's yours. Save it for his child."

CHAPTER ONE

JULY was really a lovely month in San Francisco, Amber thought as she sat on the park bench and studied the ocean she could glimpse in the distance. A steady breeze blew from the west, keeping the temperatures cool. She felt as if she were awakening from hibernation. Which, in a way she was. Jimmy's death had been so unexpected, she'd seemed to view everything through a fog. But lately, she'd started to notice things.

Like the jogger who ran into view from her left. The park had an exercise course along the jogging track. Those who wished could stop and do the exercises in the fresh air and sunshine. The station opposite the bench consisted of iron bars at various heights for chin-ups.

She'd seen the man before. He came as regular as clockwork every other day at this time. Amber wondered if she'd decided to take a break at this particular moment because of that fact. Or could she convince herself her being here was purely coincidental?

She watched him as he stopped at the bars and began a series of chin-ups. His arms were muscular and he seemed to do the pull-ups without any effort. His back and shoulder muscles rippled and moved as he pulled himself up over and over. His T-shirt was tucked into the back of the waistband of his jogging shorts leaving that golden expanse of chest and back bare. Long, muscular legs ended in running shoes.

A light sheen of perspiration coated his tanned skin. She watched as he pulled himself up at least two dozen times. When he was finished, he glanced at her. Raising his hand in silent salute, he began jogging again, soon lost from sight.

She let out a breath she hadn't known she'd held.

Wow. He could be a calendar model with those shoulders and that muscular body. She had told her friend Bets about him. She'd wanted to come to see for herself, but Amber guarded this time. She didn't want to share.

Guilt assailed her. She couldn't be interested in another man, she'd just lost her husband.

Though, she argued, she was not really *interested*, it was more of an observation of a male physique.

All right, with a quick fluttering of interest—just to prove life goes on, as her mother had said.

Ten minutes later, enough time to make sure he'd passed the next station and was well beyond sight, she rose to head for home. Her finals were finished, her second year of college completed last month. She needed to sort through her papers and toss those she'd never need again. Then she had to clean out the flat and decide what to do about living arrangements in the future. A studio flat near the university wouldn't do when the baby arrived. She knew that. But she had delayed making any decisions until school ended.

She wasn't interested in moving in with her mother and stepfather, though they had both urged her to do so. Sara and Matt had married after her own wedding to Jimmy.

Amber considered them still newlyweds. She didn't want to intrude.

Besides, she was uncomfortable around them. They were so obviously in love. She envied her mother the lavish attention she received from her new husband. Amber hadn't had that during the few months she and Jimmy had been married. He'd been too caught up in his work. And in taking her for granted.

Crossing the street from the park, she turned toward the apartment building. She'd been coming to the park since the good weather arrived. She wasn't sure when she began noticing her jogger. A couple of weeks ago maybe? Now she waited each day to see him and wonder about him. Was he also a student that he could take time to jog in the middle of the afternoon? He seemed older than most students she knew.

Maybe he had a night job and exercised before heading off to work.

Not that she should be speculating at all, she chided herself as she opened the large glass door that led to the small lobby of the building. Her husband hadn't even been dead five months. Wasn't there supposed to be a year of mourning?

Her phone was ringing when she reached her apartment and she hurried inside to answer it.

"Amber?" It was Virginia Woodworth, her mother-in-law.

"Yes, Virginia." She sank on the sofa and leaned back. Another wave of guilt swept through her. She had not yet told Virginia and James that they would be grandparents before Christmas. They would be thrilled to know there was a baby of Jimmy's on the way. She was already starting to show. So why hadn't she told them?

"Where were you? I tried calling three times. James and I want you to come to dinner tonight. James wants to discuss dismantling Jimmy's room. I think it's too soon. What do you think?"

"When the time is right, you'll know it," Amber said. Virginia asked her this question at least once a week. Amber had been spared that kind of decision in her own home. She and Jimmy had never really lived together during their brief marriage.

What kind of marriage was that?

"It's not as if we need the room for anything else. I think we should leave it the way he had it."

"He's never coming back, Virginia," she said softly.

"I know that!" Virginia's voice cracked. "I can't believe my baby's gone."

Amber heard the tears and blinked back her own. She, too, had difficulty believing she'd never see him again. During the last two years, she'd only seen him a few weeks.

And he'd changed. She'd changed.

For the first time she wondered if they had married too quickly. Her mother had said so before the wedding. Amber remembered she'd urged them to wait until Jimmy finished his tour of duty. How different would things be if they had waited?

"I can't come for dinner tonight," Amber said. "I have plans. But I suggest you wait a little longer on the room." She didn't want to get in the middle of an argument between James and Virginia. Most of the time she sided with her father-in-law, which upset Virginia. But he took a much more pragmatic view of things, which Amber liked.

"What plans?" the older woman asked quickly.

Amber sighed softly. Lately Virginia had grown more

and more demanding. She wanted to spend time with Amber—to talk about Jimmy. She resented Amber's study time and school work. When courses ended for the summer, Virginia wanted to spend even more time with Amber.

Virginia seemed to have stopped on the day Jimmy died. And she expected Amber to stop everything as well.

Amber was trying her best to move forward.

Would knowing about the baby help or not?

"Virginia, I'd like to come to dinner on Saturday. Will that work for you and James?"

She'd tell them then. She had kept it a secret long enough. She had an appointment with her obstetrician on Friday, so she'd have the latest update to share. Maybe knowing about the baby would help Virginia move on. With a new baby to plan for, she could slowly let go of her son.

"Yes. Any time, you know that Amber. We'll look for you at six on Saturday."

Amber hung up the phone and looked at the photograph of Jimmy on the table.

"Your mother is driving me crazy," she said.

There was no response.

Guilt seemed to be a constant companion lately. Amber should be grieving as hard as Virginia, but she wasn't. She felt as if she were in limbo. She missed Jimmy, no denying that. But they hadn't been as inseparable in the last year or so as they had while in high school. She had her life and he had not fit into it. He'd been in the Army, and she certainly had not tried to fit in there.

She patted her stomach, wishing her baby could have known his father. Amber's own father had deserted them when she'd been three months old. She knew how much she'd missed having a father around while growing up. But there was nothing she could do about that. At least the baby would have Matt and James. Amber hadn't even had grandparents in her life.

Rising, she went to the kitchen to get a drink of lemonade. She would have to rely on friends and her stepfather to give her baby a male role model. She didn't think she was up to getting married again any time soon. If she ever did, it would be to a man with a safe occupation like an accountant or mechanic, not someone in a dangerous field like the armed forces!

Adam Carruthers pushed himself to finish the course. The highlight of his run had been the high bars—where the pretty blonde sat on the nearby bench. He'd first noticed her a few weeks ago. She seemed to visit the park every afternoon at the same time. And he'd made sure he was at the park the same time every afternoon he could make it.

Once finished with the bars, he began to lose interest in the exercise course. He remembered her smile the first time he'd waved. He kept trying to come up with a way to meet her, but not when he was wearing jogging shorts and sweating up a storm. Twice he'd returned to that area to see if he could strike up a conversation, but she'd been gone.

She must live near the park to come so frequently. He himself had an apartment in an older building only a couple of blocks away. It was close enough to the fire station he could walk to his shifts, and inexpensive due to its proximity to the University. Several of the other tenants were students. Not that he knew many of his neighbors; he'd only moved in a few weeks earlier when he'd been transferred from the Hunter's Point station.

He retraced his steps, noting the empty bench when he passed. Maybe Friday he'd forget working out and come to meet her.

Friday Amber caught the bus to her mother's new apartment in the Marina District. Matt opened the door when she rang the bell and gave her a quick hug.

"How are you doing?" he asked.

"Fine. How's Mom?"

"Also fine. She has more energy now that she's into the next trimester."

Amber smiled. Matt was thrilled about the new baby he and her mother were expecting. He would accompany them to the doctor's. She and her mother had decided to use the same obstetrician and had moved into a schedule that let them make their checkups at the same time. Matt often accompanied Sara, which had Amber feeling left out. But she still liked going with them. If Sara had the first appointment, sometimes Matt left afterward and Sara came in with Amber.

"Hi, honey," her mother said, joining them. She gave her a hug and kiss on the cheek.

"I hope I didn't keep you waiting long," Sara said, giving her husband a private smile.

Amber looked away. She had a good idea what they'd been doing to keep her mother so long. Envy struck again. She was delighted for her mother. It was way past time for her to find happiness with someone. Amber just wished she could have had that, too. She felt as if she hadn't been part of a couple in a long time. The short honeymoon and few weeks Jimmy had been on temporary duty stateside didn't count.

"We want to go to lunch afterward, is that okay with you?" Sara asked.

"I'll head for home, if it's all the same. Time's a little tight." Lunch would put her back too late to see her jogger today. And if he kept to the schedule, it would be Sunday before she saw him again.

"We'll run you home afterward," Matt said. "Save you riding the bus."

"Okay." She'd keep track of the time and make sure she was back early enough.

For a moment it struck her as funny she made such a big deal out of seeing a stranger from a distance for about ten minutes. But it had been so long since she wanted to do much of anything, she hoped this was a good sign.

She'd have to ask Bets. She wasn't sure she wanted her mother to know she was ogling strange men.

"I'm planning to tell Virginia and James about the baby tomorrow night," Amber said a short time later from the back seat of the new minivan Matt had bought for her mother. His sports car would not be suitable for a family, he'd declared. After a quick lunch, Matt would then drive her to her apartment.

"They'll be thrilled," Sara said, looking over her shoulder at her daughter. "Of course Virginia will want to know why you didn't tell her earlier. But James will simply be happy to hear the news."

"I'm hoping it'll give Virginia something to think about beside Jimmy. It's hard dealing with her, Mom. All she wants to do is look at old photographs, and talk about every aspect of his life. I know how well he did in school, what sports he played, who his friends were. I was there. But sometimes I think she doesn't remember that."

"It's hard for her, Amber. She's trying to hold on as best

she knows how. Time will help. And the news about the baby," Sara said gently.

"Want to go shopping with us tomorrow?" Matt asked. "We're going to check out cribs, changers, rocking chairs and other paraphernalia your mother assures me a newborn needs."

Amber smiled and shook her head. "I'll probably be getting my things from the secondhand store. But not yet. I have nowhere to store anything in my apartment. I have to move. Now that school is out, I need to concentrate on finding another place. Thank goodness Jimmy's insurance covers everything for a while. I don't know what kind of job I'd be able to get five months pregnant."

"You're not getting anything in a secondhand store," Matt said. "Doting grandparents to the forefront." He smiled at Sara. "We want to buy the baby's furnishings."

"I can't let you do that," Amber said.

"Sure you can, sweetie," her mother replied, reaching out to touch Matt's hand. "We want to. There's no reason to say no. You just have to pick out what you want."

Amber was overwhelmed by their generosity. She blinked back tears. "Let me get an apartment first."

"I still have the one we lived in. You could move there," Sara suggested tentatively.

"Mom, you moved out of it a couple of months ago. Why are you still holding on to that place?"

Sara was silent for a moment, then looked at Amber. "Because of rent control, and how long we lived there, the rates are low. I wondered if you'd like to move in after I heard about Jimmy. I didn't want to pressure you in any way, but it does have two bedrooms, it's on the bus line, and you know where everything is. It's a nice neighborhood. Still no pressure, but think about it."

"I will." She swallowed the lump in her throat. Her mother had always taken such great care of her. Would she be able to take such good care of her baby? Her mother had been left alone with her newborn when her husband abandoned them. Her parents had never helped. Amber was far better off with her mother and Matt to offer support. And she knew Virginia and James would help out for Jimmy's sake.

She could do this. She'd love her child and raise him or her to be the best person possible. And tell them stories of their father. Jimmy would have loved children.

Amber made sure she was at the park early. The doctor's appointment had reassured her everything was progressing normally. She'd taken a battery of tests, normal procedures these days. She was scheduled for another sonogram in a few weeks. So far she'd held off finding out the gender of her baby. She had until then to decide if she wanted to wait until it was born.

She was showing, but not a lot. Her appetite hadn't been that robust after hearing about Jimmy. The doctor had said everything was fine. She could still wear some of her clothes, but soon would be forced into maternity attire.

Sitting on the park bench, she leaned back, letting the hot sun shine on her face. She felt happier than she had since she'd received the news about Jimmy. In only a few months she'd have a new baby to love and raise, and a new brother or sister to get to know. And if her baby was born first, it would be older than its aunt or uncle. How weird was that?

She waited. Time moved slowly. She looked down the path. No jogger.

A young mother pushed a toddler in a stroller. Birds sang in the trees. The breeze was missing today, it was hotter than it had been earlier in the week.

Still Amber waited. She checked her watch. He hadn't come earlier, had he? She thought she'd been here with time to spare. But as the minutes slowly ticked by, she knew she wasn't going to see the man today.

The disappointment was surprising. She didn't even know his name. She knew nothing about him. Yet, she waited with anticipation each day to see him.

A half hour later she gave up. Would he come tomorrow instead? She'd be here just in case. She had time before her dinner engagement with the Woodworths.

CHAPTER TWO

AMBER was feeling almost sick by the time she arrived at the Woodworths' home Saturday afternoon. She'd been lucky to miss the morning sickness that her mother experienced from time to time. She hadn't gained much weight. Even the tiredness her mother felt wasn't a problem.

But telling Jimmy's parents had her so nervous she was stressed to the max.

Virginia greeted her sadly, hugging her for a long moment, as if capturing some of her son through Amber.

James waited for his hug, then ushered her into the living room.

"At loose ends now that summer is half over?" he asked when they were seated. Virginia hovered about, pouring iced tea.

"Not really. I have a lot to plan for," Amber said.

"School starts up again in September, what will you do until then?" Virginia asked.

"Sit down, please, Virginia, I have something to tell you," Amber said. She had rehearsed what she'd say over and over. Why was she feeling so defensive? They would be delighted with the news.

Virginia perched on the edge of the sofa beside her husband, looking worried. "What is it?"

"I'm pregnant. I'm going to have a baby in November. You two will be grandparents," Amber said quickly.

The older couple stared at her.

"Pregnant?" James said.

"With Jimmy's baby?" Virginia asked, a spark of enthusiasm showing for the first time in months. "Why didn't you tell us before? How long have you known? How are you feeling? Oh, James. We are going to be grandparents. I never expected this when we heard the terrible news."

James hugged his wife and smiled at Amber.

"That is wonderful, honey."

"Why didn't you tell us sooner?" Virginia asked, struggling to free herself from her husband's embrace. "You must have known before today. Did Jimmy know?"

Amber shook her head. "I didn't know the last time I spoke with him. I never had a chance to tell him."

"But you had a chance to tell us before now," Virginia said waspishly. "Why haven't you told us before today?"

"Dear, the important thing is we know now," James said, a hint of warning in his tone.

"When is it due? We have such plans to make. You should move in with us, dear, rather than stay in that poky little apartment where you're living. There's lots of room here. You have no room for a baby in your place. You can have the guest room and the baby can have Jimmy's room."

"Thank you, Virginia. I appreciate the offer, but I do have options. My mother and Matt have invited me to live with them—"

"Ridiculous. Your mother is expecting a new baby herself. She'll have enough to deal with without a second infant. I insist."

"Actually, I also have another choice. For the time being, I'm thinking of moving back into our old apartment. It has two bedrooms, one for me and one for the baby when it comes. And it'll be close to both you and Mom."

"I won't hear of it. I insist you move in with us. Do you know if it's a boy or girl yet? We'll have to get new furniture, we didn't keep Jimmy's baby things, did we, James?" Virginia jumped up, a list of things she wanted to do tumbling forth.

Amber watched, bemused. She had hoped for some enthusiasm, some indication Virginia could move on, but this was getting out of hand. She had no intention of living with Jimmy's parents. And despite the plans Virginia was making, Amber was the mother of the baby. She would decide where she lived and the furniture she wanted.

James picked up on Amber's silence. "Virginia, let's discuss this further over dinner. I think we are all hungry."

"How can you think about food? James—we're going to be grandparents!"

"But not tonight. We invited Amber for dinner, let's feed the girl."

Amber tuned Virginia out through much of the meal. The older woman needed no response to her verbal list-making. She would have the child's life planned through college, if Amber allowed it. Let the woman dream. It was better than more recent thoughts. Time enough for Amber to let Virginia know what she would be doing. Nothing had to be decided tonight.

She wondered how Jimmy would have viewed a baby. They had not discussed children. He had been focused on his work in the Army. When they married, she'd wanted to finish college and begin teaching before starting a family. Would he have been happy to have a baby so early?

Not that it would have had the impact on his life it did on hers.

If she budgeted carefully, could she still take classes? Maybe her mother or Virginia would watch the baby while she finished school. Long before the child was ready for kindergarten, she'd have her degree and be ready to teach.

Amber came back to the present when Virginia's voice stopped. She looked at her.

"Did you hear a word I said?" Virginia asked, with a trace of frustration.

"I'm afraid I was thinking about the future. I hope I can get my teaching credentials by the time the baby is ready for school. It would be the perfect job. I'll be home summers and holidays and not need childcare except for a few hours a day."

"Nonsense. You have no need to work. We can take care of you and Jimmy's child."

"I don't plan to be a stay-at-home mother," Amber said, remembering her own mother had worked. They had always been close despite the hours apart. And Amber thought she had a pretty terrific childhood to remember.

"Maybe you should consider letting us raise the child," Virginia said slowly. "You're young, have your whole life ahead of you. We can raise him. Tell him about his daddy. You go get your job."

Amber shook her head. "I'll raise my own child. But I do hope his grandparents will be an integral part of his or her life."

Amber left as soon as she felt she could politely do

so once dinner was finished. She didn't want to rock the boat with her relations with the Woodworths, but she was tired of Virginia's assumption she'd play a major role in her child's future. She would be one of two grand-mothers. And of the two, Amber would count on her own mother more.

She called her friend Bets when she got home.

"How'd it go?" Bets asked when she heard Amber's voice.

"Virginia is obsessing on the baby now. She even asked me to let her raise the baby."

"She misses Jimmy. Stand tough."

"I plan to."

"So, did you see your friend?"

"What friend?" Amber suspected she knew who Bets meant, but she played dumb.

"Oh yeah, like you have a lot of secret friends."

"I don't even know the man."

"So take him some water. It's got to be hot work show-ing off to the ladies, offer him some next time."

Amber laughed. Never in a million years could she en-vision herself doing such a thing.

"Bets, I'm not looking to meet him. I just enjoy look-ing at him."

"Hon, you didn't die when Jimmy did. You need to find yourself another hunk and move on."

"He hasn't been dead that long."

"But he's been gone forever. I never even met the man and we've been friends for almost two years."

Amber acknowledged the fact. When Jimmy had flown home for a few weeks' temporary duty in San Francisco, they'd rushed to get married. Bets had been invited to the wedding, but had been unable to attend. The few times

Jimmy was available after that, Amber had selfishly wanted his attention, not to share him with friends.

"I'm not looking to become part of a couple again any time soon," Amber said.

"Fine. Give it a little longer. But don't shut yourself away just because Jimmy died. It's the pits, don't get me wrong. But you're too young to stay a widow the rest of your life. Want to go to the show tomorrow afternoon?"

Amber was tempted. But Sunday was a jogging day.

"Maybe later in the week."

They chatted for a little longer, then Amber said goodbye. She couldn't believe she was turning down a guaranteed fun afternoon with her friend on the off chance she'd get to briefly glimpse a man she didn't even know.

The next afternoon Amber went to the park early. She hoped her jogger showed today. She wanted something to take her mind off the confrontation with her mother-in-law. Virginia had already called once today, suggesting Amber come over to discuss things. The baby wasn't due for another four months, but Virginia was anxious to make plans.

Once again her jogger didn't appear. Had he stopped exercising? Maybe he had worked a night shift and his hours had been changed. Or maybe he was a student and had gone home for part of the summer.

Whatever the reason, Amber was disappointed that she hadn't seen him.

Instead of craving ice cream and pickles while pregnant, was she getting fixated on a stranger? She wanted her fix of seeing the man, admiring his body as he exercised, maybe even fantasizing about meeting him one day.

Like he'd be at all interested in a pregnant woman who,

if her mother was to be believed, would soon look and feel like a walrus.

Not that she wanted someone interested in her. Not exactly. But she was lonely. Had been for more than a year. Brief e-mails from Jimmy hadn't done much to alleviate that feeling when he'd been alive. Now she didn't even have that.

After three more visits to the park, Amber was ready to give up her quest. The man was obviously not running in the early afternoons anymore. She had to find something else to do at one.

Saturday afternoon was a busy time at the park. There were little children chasing each other around. More people used the jogging path and exercise equipment. An elderly couple strolled along the grassy edge, talking quietly.

She watched as squirrels ran up the trees. The sun was too hot to sit in for long. Maybe she'd take a walk along the path for some mild exercise. She had only packing to look forward to when she returned to her apartment.

"Hi."

She looked up, and blinked in surprise. Her jogger was standing right in front of her, fully clothed, with his arm in a sling.

"Hi. I missed you, were you in an accident?" she asked, taking in the cast on his arm, and burns along his neck and cheek.

He sat beside her. "Slight altercation with a recalcitrant fire. Can't run for a while."

Amber felt fluttery as he leaned against the wooden back. She'd never even waved to him when he waved to her. Now she'd told him she missed him. How dumb was that? But embarrassment didn't explain the tingling feeling that swept through her. He sat too close, taking up her space. She was more aware of him than she'd ever been when he'd been wearing jogging shorts. How had he managed to steal the very air she was trying to breathe?

"I'm sorry," she said. The burns didn't look too bad, but were still red and blistered. "What happened to your arm?"

Keep it friendly and normal, she thought. Her gaze was drawn to his mouth. To lips that were firmly shaped and moved enticingly as he talked.

"Broke it when I fell through a floor. I'll be good to go in a few weeks. Until then, no chin-ups." He nodded toward the bars.

"Or jogging, either, I expect," she said, smiling at him. A warm glow began to replace the flutters. *He'd stopped to talk to her.*

"I'm Adam Carruthers," he said, offering a hand.

"Amber Woodworth," she said, taking it. "Was it your house that burned?" She withdrew her hand, clenching it into a fist. His palm had been warm, hard, as if callused. His dark eyes looked directly into hers. Somewhere she heard the background noise of the children, but she felt detached—cocooned alone with Adam Carruthers.

"Not mine. I'm a firefighter. We were trying to save an old building off Masonic. The fire had too much of a hold on it. We lost it."

"Oh. That's a dangerous field. I'm glad you weren't badly injured." A firefighter—that would explain his ability to exercise in midafternoon. Didn't they work alternating days?

"Do you come to the park often?" he asked.

"Almost every day. I'm going to miss it." Miss you.

"But I'm moving soon. There isn't a park near my new place," she said. Time to end this. There was no future in a friendship. Before long, she'd be back at the apartment across town she and her mother had shared. Adam would still be living in this section of the city. It was unlikely they'd have any reason to run into each other.

She'd miss watching him, though.

She rose. "I'm glad you're going to be all right."

He stood beside her. "When are you moving?"

"End of the month, or early next. My lease is up the end of August and I'm not renewing. I've got to go now. Goodbye." She had to leave before she thought up a bunch of reasons to stay in touch, to return to the park in the afternoons and watch as he ran past showing more skin than was good for her equilibrium.

"I'll walk with you," he said, falling into step.

"My apartment isn't far. I don't need an escort. Goodbye."

"Goodbye, Amber Woodworth."

She turned and walked out of the park. Waiting at the traffic light, she noticed he'd followed her and was standing a couple of paces behind her. When the signal turned, she hurried across the street and turned toward her place. She could hear his footsteps behind her.

Turning, she stopped and put her hands on her hips. "Are you following me?"

"Now that sort of depends on your point of view," he said, stopping a few yards away. Even from that distance, Amber could see the mocking amusement in his eyes.

"What does that mean?" she asked suspiciously.

"You're going in the direction I'm headed, so if my walking behind you is following you, then, yes I am. On the other hand, if you turn off before I do, and I keep going, then no, I'm not following you."

"You go first," she said. He didn't look dangerous, but one never knew. Though she didn't feel threatened by a man with a broken arm. Or one who seemed to be laughing at her.

The amusement in his eyes irritated her. She waited for him to walk past, then began following him. At the next intersection, he turned onto her street. How had he known where she lived?

He glanced back when he was partway down and when she turned onto the street, he called, "Are you following me?"

At least she lived in a secure building. He couldn't get inside unless she let him in.

"No, I live in that building." She pointed to one ahead of them.

He looked at it, then back at her. "I live there, top floor, right side."

That information startled her. Was it true?

"Are you a student?" he asked.

She nodded.

"Figures. There are a lot of students in the building. Pleased to meet you, neighbor." He turned and headed to the building. When he drew near the bank of mailboxes, he pointed to one. She stepped closer and read the name: A. Carruthers.

He moved his finger along the names and stopped by hers, A. Woodworth. Then he opened the lobby door with his key, holding it for her.

Amber stepped by him to enter, smelling a woodsy scent as she passed. Her heart raced. Her mind wanted to explore this connection just a little more. What could it hurt? She wasn't moving away for a couple of weeks. To be friends with someone didn't mean a lifelong connection.

"Thank you," she said and walked to the small elevator. He stayed by the door, watching her with those amused eyes. "Is it following you if I ride up the elevator in the same car?"

"A woman can't be too careful," she said primly. Wouldn't her mother be proud of her?

The amusement left. "You're absolutely right. If I make you uncomfortable, ride up alone. I'll wait."

"Don't be silly. Come on. I'm on the fourth floor, left side in a studio."

Amber wondered if she'd made a mistake when the elevator doors slid shut. Adam seemed to fill the space in the small car. She tried to ignore the sensations that began to clamor inside, the fluttery feeling had returned. She wanted to check her hair, make sure her lipstick was still on. The loose top she wore camouflaged her blossoming figure. Would he have noticed? She noticed every thing about him, from the crinkles near his eyes, to the over six foot height, to the trimmed dark hair, worn longer than Army regulations.

She was more conscious of him beside her than she expected. Bets would say something, do something to end the awkwardness. But Amber remained tongue-tied.

Fortunately the elevator lumbered to her floor and stopped. When the doors opened, Adam reached out to hold them from closing as she stepped out.

"Want to meet on the roof for a drink later?" he asked.

The building had a flat roof, a portion of which had been covered with wooden decking and a railing. The landlord allowed tenants to bring their own chairs and tables and use it as a private garden area. Amber had loved that feature when she rented the apartment last summer.

"Amber, where have you been?" Virginia came down the hall. "I've been waiting more than twenty minutes. I didn't expect you to be away from home." Virginia gave Adam a sharp look.

"Who is this?"

"This is Adam Carruthers—a neighbor. Adam, Virginia Woodworth."

"Her mother-in-law," Virginia said quickly. "Come along, Amber, I have some catalogs to show you."

Adam watched as Amber turned to walk away with the harridan who had accosted them. Feeling poleaxed, he stepped back inside the elevator and pushed the button for his floor.

He hadn't known she was married! He tried to remember if there was a ring on her finger. Surely he would have noticed.

Even if he hadn't, what was she doing flirting with strange men when she had a husband?

He was disappointed in the fact she was unavailable. Not that he was looking for a lifelong commitment, just a friendly neighbor to hang out with from time to time.

And if he'd wanted to explore where this sexual awareness might lead, well, that was normal. But not if she was married. He didn't mess with other men's wives.

He let himself into his apartment. So much for trying to find out more about the lady who seemed mesmerized by his body. He'd been deluding himself. Or maybe he'd totally misread the situation. For all he knew, she'd hadn't been watching him but mentally compiling a grocery list. Laughing wryly, he headed for the kitchen.

He'd get a cold soda and head for the roof. Nothing else to do. They'd released him from the hospital yesterday. He was on medical leave from the department until he got an okay from the doctor. Which would be in about six weeks when his arm healed and he could pass the physical.

So what was he going to do for that long?

"Where were you?" Virginia persisted as Amber unlocked her door.

"I went for a walk to the park. As I do most days," she said. "What are you doing here?"

"I came to see you. Can't a woman visit her daughter-in-law?" Virginia said defensively.

"Of course. I didn't expect you, however. Otherwise I would have stayed home until you arrived. Have a seat. Would you like something to drink?" If Virginia hadn't been here, would Amber now be on the roof with Adam sharing a cold drink?

"I'll take iced tea if you have it. Who was that man?"

"A neighbor. He lives on one of the upper floors." Amber quickly prepared the beverage for Virginia. She took some water for herself and went to sit beside the older woman.

"What did you bring?" She stifled a sigh. She hoped Virginia wasn't going to prove difficult. She wanted to decide for herself what she and her baby would be doing, not fall into Virginia's wishes without comment.

Virginia pulled a catalog from her purse, opening it to a double page spread of baby furniture. "I got this from the baby store. They have lots of furniture on display, but this gives the full range. I thought that was nice," she said, pointing to a fancy French provincial baby set.

Amber closed the catalog and handed it to Virginia. "I

told you, my mother and Matt are buying the baby's bedroom furnishings."

"We're the baby's grandparents, too. I want to do something. Your mother doesn't need to do this. She has her own baby coming. I have no one. I'm buying the crib."

How did Amber handle this? She didn't want to hurt Jimmy's mother. But the woman was driving her crazy.

"Virginia, we don't need to do anything today. I've got to move and get settled before I'll be ready to think about acquiring more furniture. We'll have time to discuss all this after I've moved."

"I don't see anything to discuss," Virginia said in a huff.

"There'll be lots of things to talk about. But not today."

"Amber, you are just putting off the inevitable. Time goes by so quickly. Before you know it, you'll have the baby here and not be ready. I say get prepared early."

"I will, I promise. Where is James today?"

"He went to play golf."

"Maybe you should take up the game."

"I hardly think so," Virginia said, not at all mollified by Amber's attempts to defuse the situation.

What her mother-in-law needed was a hobby, Amber thought. Something to take her mind off her lost son, and the coming baby. She had never worked outside the home, though Amber thought she was a member of some women's club.

"Did that man know you were married?" Virginia asked suddenly.

Amber looked at her. It struck her—

"Technically, I am not married, Virginia," she said slowly. She had never really felt married. They'd had a lovely honeymoon the week after the wedding, then five other nights scattered across several weeks before Jimmy had left. They had never gone grocery shopping together, argued over which television show to watch, or had friends to dinner.

"What do you mean? Of course you're married." Virginia looked shocked.

"Actually, the vows were until death parted us," Amber said gently.

"So you're dating again?" Her shocked tone couldn't have been worse.

"I am not! Virginia, the man rode up in the elevator with me. He's a neighbor, nothing more."

"He asked you for a drink, I heard him."

"A neighbor being friendly. You're making too much of this."

"Come stay with James and me. Your mother is busy, school is finished for the year. You don't need either apartment. We have plenty of room."

"I'm not going to move in with you, Virginia. Thank you for the offer, but I moved out from Mom's when I went to college. I'm grown up now and I like being on my own. Please stop pressuring me about this." Amber wasn't sure what she had to do to keep Virginia from trying to take over her life, but she'd do whatever it took.

"Well, if offering you a home is pressure, I'm sure I didn't mean it." She rose and snatched up the catalog. "I'll see myself out."

Which didn't mean much, Amber thought with a hint of amusement. The apartment was a single large room, with an area for a kitchen and a private bath.

She felt bad for Virginia, but knew she needed to stand firm or the woman would take over her life.

"She needs a hobby," Amber said to herself once Virginia had gone. "What would fill her need to be needed?" Something beside her grandchild!

A half hour later, Amber rode the elevator to the roof. She stepped out onto the decking, looking around. There was no one else in sight. She refused to admit she was disappointed.

She walked to one of the chairs she'd left up here and sat down. She'd miss this feature when she moved back to the apartment she'd grown up in. There was no park nearby, nor a rooftop garden.

The sun was still warm, but there was more of a breeze. The bright sparkling water of the Pacific could be seen. She loved this feature about the apartment building.

But she wouldn't be far from the marina and the wharf or Fort Mason in the other flat, so there'd be plenty of places to walk.

Only none would have Adam Carruthers.

She remembered the amusement in his eyes when he looked at her. Slowly she smiled. He was a good-looking man, even when he wore clothes. Had it been hard to get dressed one-handed? It was probably difficult to prepare food.

Maybe, as a good neighborly gesture, she should prepare dinner for him tonight. She could make something easy to eat one-handed, and take it up around six. No one could find fault with that, could they? It was a neighborly thing to do.

CHAPTER THREE

EXACTLY at six o'clock, Amber rang the bell for apartment 5C. The shepherd's pie had turned out perfectly. It was an easy meal to prepare, and easy to eat without needing to use a knife.

Adam opened the door, obviously surprised to see her.

"I thought it might be difficult to cook, so I made you this," she said brightly, holding out the covered plate.

He looked at the plate then at her for a long moment.

"Thank you, that's kind of you."

He stood aside and gestured for her to enter.

Amber stepped inside the apartment and looked around. It was sparsely furnished, with few pictures on the walls. Those that had been hung were photographs of white water rivers and soaring mountains. She liked the bold, clean lines of the room.

He pointed to the dining table near the window. "I usually eat there. Is it hot, or do I need to warm it up?"

"Do you have a microwave?"

He nodded.

"You might wish to put it in for a couple of minutes. I just dished it up, but it cooled coming up here."

"Nice of you to take the time. I'd invite you to stay, but I guess your husband will expect you right back."

She looked at him. "My husband was killed several months ago, overseas. He was in the Army."

"God, I'm sorry. I didn't know that. From what that woman said earlier, I expected him to be waiting in the apartment."

"A studio would be cramped quarters for two," she said. Turning she reached for the doorknob. "I hope you enjoy the meal."

"Wait." He reached the door at the same time and held it shut. "Join me, unless you have other plans. Is your mother-in-law still downstairs?"

"She left shortly after she arrived." Amber hesitated. She hadn't expected an invitation. Yet, why not? He was alone, so was she. A meal together would be a change from the lonely meals she'd eaten during the last months.

"Okay. I'll run down and get my plate and be right back."

Adam waited by the door. He felt like he was on a roller coaster. First he thought she was single, then learned she was married. Only she wasn't still married, she was a widow. She couldn't be more than twenty or twenty-one. Hell of a deal to be widowed so young.

He was sorry for the husband. But he was not sorry she was single again. How long ago had the husband died? Was she starting to date again? He wanted to be first in line if that was the case.

Glancing at the cast, he shook his head. Who would have thought being laid up was a way to get attention?

She was back in only a moment, smiling shyly. Reminding himself they'd just met and she hadn't a clue to the fantasies he'd woven starring the two of them, he vowed to take things slowly.

The meal was delicious. And so he told her.

"I'm glad you like it," she replied. "Can you cook?"

"Enough to get by, but not with this," he said, raising the cast. "Maybe in another week or two, but right now my arm aches too much to use it. I was planning to order in."

"That's fun, once in a while."

"Not as good as home cooking," he agreed. "So what course work are you taking at the University?"

"I want to be a primary school teacher. I've just finished my second year, so I still have a long way to go."

"Good job choice. Teachers are underrated, I've always thought."

She smiled at him, and Adam felt a spark of awareness shoot right to the center. She should smile more often; she was beautiful when she did.

"I think so, too. And they can make such a difference at the early stages of education. I want all my students to love to learn, and achieve great things."

And everyone would probably do his or her best if they received a smile from the teacher. He would, for sure.

"Just as I want that for my baby," she finished.

Adam stared at her. "You're pregnant?" He looked at her. She didn't look pregnant. Maybe a little pudgy around the waist, but he'd been more interested in her blue eyes and bright smile than taking inventory of her figure.

"Yes, I'm almost five months along. Which makes it doubly hard not to have a husband and father for the baby. I wish that was different."

Being pregnant was worse than being married. Married,

she was off limits. Being pregnant and a widow, she suddenly took on a new look. Did her comment mean she would welcome a new husband and father for her baby? Was she on the prowl for a man?

"I don't do happy ever after," he blurted out.

"Pardon me?" She stared at him in surprise.

"I'm not looking for any kind of long-term relationship." Might as well be upfront about everything.

"Neither am I," Amber said, pushing back her chair. "Did you think I was coming on to you? I was just making a neighborly gesture bringing supper, not looking for some kind of relationship. I lost my husband only a few months ago. What kind of person do you think I am? I'm not looking for some substitute for Jimmy. And even if I were, the last person I'd choose would be another man in a dangerous occupation. If I ever get married again, which I doubt, it'll be to some nice guy who's an accountant or salesman where the most dangerous thing he does is drive to work each day!"

"Hey, you said you wished that was different. What would any man think?" he protested.

"That a neighbor offered to help him out when he hurt his arm," she retorted, rising and taking her plate, and reaching over for his. She looked into his eyes, fire sparking from her own. "I didn't realize your ego was so monumental you'd misinterpret an act of kindness for a come-on. But thank you for expanding my education. I'm always ready for that. I won't make such a gesture again any time soon."

He hadn't finished the meal, but she snatched up the plate and headed for the door.

"Wait."

But this time Amber Woodworth didn't wait a heartbeat. One moment she was storming away, the next gone.

Adam groaned aloud. He'd made a total mess of the evening. She'd been kind enough to bring him dinner and he acted like she had been hunting him down. He was an idiot. He rubbed his face with his good hand, wincing when he touched the burned skin.

He hated relationships. He could certainly understand her reluctance to get involved with anyone doing what he did. Casual dating was all he was good for. And after this fiasco, he wasn't sure he was even good for that.

He'd been so surprised to learn she was pregnant. Not that that excused his outburst. She had never given him a sign she was interested in him in any special way. Was his ego as inflated as she said that he expected every woman to have her own private get-Adam-married agenda?

Now he had to do the apology bit—and he hated that.

But he couldn't let her leave without some explanation. The irony of it all struck him as he headed downstairs. He hoped she'd listen to his apology.

Amber was so angry she'd like to spit. How dare that arrogant male think she had some designs on him when she was only trying to be helpful? As she scraped the remnants of dinner from their plates, she thought of a half dozen other scathing comments she should have blasted him with.

When she heard the bell ring, she paused. If it was Virginia again, she didn't know if she'd be able to keep a civil facade. She was angry and not in any hurry to get over it. Woe to anyone crossing her now.

Opening the door, she saw Adam. She slammed it

shut—only, quick reflexes prevailed and he caught it with his good hand, pushing it open.

"I'm sorry," he said.

The simple words dissipated some of the anger. He looked contrite. And good enough to eat.

That she'd even think that for a second spiked her anger again—this time toward herself.

"Fine. Goodbye." She pushed against the door.

He held it open.

"Let me explain. I know I came across sounding like a first-class jerk."

"You did." She crossed her arms, resigned to listening to some half-baked excuse for his acting the way he did. Was she supposed to forgive all and fall into his arms when he was done? Not likely! Her anger grew when she realized she was fighting the notion. Did she really want to fall into his arms?

"No one ever says anything, but I can see for myself what people do. My mother did."

"Your mother did what?"

"Tried to find a husband. My father abandoned her, she had me to raise. She wanted help. A natural enough desire. I think two parents are needed to raise a child."

"There are a lot of single parents, men and women, raising children just fine, thank you." She would not hear a word against her own mother.

"I know. But there are some who could do a whole lot better with a mate to share the responsibilities. So my immediate reaction to hearing you were pregnant was that you were on a husband hunt."

"I had a husband. He died. I don't need another."

"Amber, you're young. You'll change your mind."

She shrugged. "So you're sorry you leaped to conclusions based on your mother's husband hunt. Fine. Apology accepted. Shut the door behind you."

She returned to the kitchenette, struck by the similarities between Adam and her. Both had been raised by single mothers. But hers had not been out husband hunting. Sara had gotten an education, went to work and provided Amber with a terrific childhood. They might not have had a lot of material things, but they'd had what counted—love.

"So do we have a truce?" Adam asked.

She spun around. "I thought you left."

"You said close the door behind me, didn't say which side I should be on. No wonder you're moving, this place is small, especially if you're having a baby. I'm amazed you could cook for two. You should see the size of my kitchen in comparison. I'll never complain about it again."

"Why are you still here? You gave your apology, I accepted. End of discussion."

"Is it? Don't women usually harp on things long after they've passed?"

"More of your mother?"

"Girlfriends over the years."

"I'm not your girlfriend, not do I plan to be." She didn't want anything more to do with the man. How dare he think she was on some kind of husband hunt just because she cooked him a meal?

"Great. I'm not in the running for being a husband."

Amber stared at him suspiciously. "So that's settled. You can leave now."

"Fine. Thanks again for dinner. Maybe I'll run into you on the roof one day."

His tone suggested if he did, he'd probably push her off.

"Maybe. I go there sometimes. I need to take advantage of it since I won't have a rooftop garden at my new place." He couldn't scare her away from the roof just because he would be there.

"When are you moving? Maybe I can help."

"I have my own help."

"Just trying to be neighborly," he said.

"Right, or trying to get rid of me sooner. I'm here for another couple of weeks." She tilted her chin, glaring at him. She couldn't believe he'd thought she was chasing after him. With his attitude, no wonder he wasn't married. Who would have him?

He turned and went to the door, pausing as he opened it. "Thanks for dinner. I enjoyed what I had of it."

She raised her finger and shook it in front of him. "Don't blame me for that. If you hadn't come out with that totally inappropriate comment, you could have finished the meal. Remember that next time."

"You'll make a terrific teacher, you already have the finger down pat."

He gave her a two-finger salute and left.

Amber stood bemused. Her anger had fled. She almost laughed at his last comment.

Once she finished cleaning the kitchen, Amber went to call her mother.

"What's up?" Sara asked when she heard her daughter's voice.

"Nothing much. I wanted to go look at the old apartment tomorrow, if that's okay. You took most of the furnishings, right? What do I need to get?"

"We'll meet you there in the afternoon and go over things," Sara suggested. "Virginia called."

Amber sat on the sofa and leaned back, gazing at the ceiling. "About me living with them?" she guessed.

"She said it would be the best solution."

"We don't have a problem needing a solution. I'm all set. I did think to ask her to watch the baby some when I'm back in school, but now I don't know. Mom, she said she wanted to raise the baby herself, as if I want to go off somewhere and not be bothered. I love this baby. I haven't even held it yet, but know I'll love it forever. I'm not giving it up even to its grandparents."

"Give her some time."

"Like I have a choice. She's always coming over. When I move back to the other apartment, she'll only be a few blocks away. Maybe I should tell her I'm dating again," she grumbled.

"What's that? Dating?"

"She saw me with a neighbor and leaped to conclusions. If only she'd seen Adam tonight, all her fears would have been dispelled. The man thinks the world revolves around him and that every female in creation wants to marry him," she grumbled.

Her mother was silent.

"Mom?"

"Who is Adam?"

"A neighbor, he lives upstairs somewhere. I just met him at the park today." No need to burden her mother with the weeks of watching him. She had only met him today.

"Young and single?"

"Of course. And I have it on good authority he plans to stay that way. He thought just because I made dinner that I was after him. Especially after he learned I was pregnant."

Sara insisted on hearing the full story. Amber had trouble relating everything without giving away her trips to the park to watch him when he exercised. That part sounded too needy.

"Do you think I should stay home and not go anywhere for a while?" she asked. "I mean, I'm not mourning Jimmy like maybe I should."

"As to that, people mourn differently. I'm not sure there is a single correct way to mourn. Or a single time span that encompasses everything."

"Did you mourn my father's leaving?" Amber asked.

"In a way. But I think I was so angry at him, and so scared, the mourning was more for the way of life I had thought we'd share than anything else."

"That's the way I feel sometimes. That we never even had a start on a life together. We went steady in high school, then he left for the Army. He wasn't the same when he was here in February."

"As people mature, they do so at different rates. Maybe he went one way and you another."

"You've said we should have waited."

"Maybe. Maybe not. No one expected him to be killed. I think you have to decide how you want to face the future and not waste time lamenting the past," Sara said. "And that will include dating and possibly falling for some other guy."

"And if I ever do, he'll have a safe job where I won't have to worry he'll go off and get himself killed," Amber said with spirit.

"Um, sounds like a plan. What does your neighbor do?"

"He's a firefighter. He broke his arm fighting a fire last week, and it's in a cast."

"So he's not in the running."

"Mom, I'm not looking for anyone right now. I have enough with the baby and school and all."

"We'll meet you at the apartment tomorrow afternoon and decide what you need to get going. Still want to go shopping for baby things next week?"

"I'd like to see what's out there. But don't tell Virginia, she wants to buy everything. I know she's a grandmother, but she's never been close with me and I don't see this as a bonding time."

"Just be patient. You're her last link to Jimmy until the baby comes."

"I guess. What are you and Matt doing tonight?"

"We're getting ready to eat dinner, then, gee, I don't know. I'm sure we'll find something to do," Sara said vaguely.

Amber laughed. "You go, Mom! But don't tell me everything. I'm still the child."

"Honey, you've grown up fast. But some X-rated things are still too much for my baby girl's ears."

Amber hung up a few minutes later, glad for the happiness in her mother's voice. But once the connection was broken, she was enveloped by a wave of loneliness. There was no one special for her anymore.

She had friends she could call, but it wasn't the same. Kathy was pregnant, but happily married. Bets was great, but not suffering from loneliness or a lack of dates.

Was she the only person in the city home alone tonight?

No, there was at least one other—the insufferable man in 5C who did not want to be married.

Cheered by the thought, she headed for the bathroom. A long soak in a hot tub would be just the way to get relaxed before bed.

* * *

Sunday Amber spent the early part of the afternoon with her mother at their old apartment. They planned the furniture she wanted for the baby, and one or two other things she would need to get to furnish the rest of the apartment.

"So have you thought of baby names yet?" Sara asked as they measured some of the windows for which Amber wanted new curtains.

"No. I thought I should check with Virginia to see if there are any family names or something. If it's a boy, I could call him James after his father and grandfather."

"Have you decided whether or not to find out the sex of the baby at our next appointment?" Sara asked.

"Have you?"

She nodded. "We've discussed it endlessly. Matt really wants to know. I guess it'll be fun to know ahead of time. We can decorate accordingly, and not be stuck with yellow or green. I didn't know with you. You were a surprise."

"I'm sort of hoping for a girl," Amber said. "It would be easier on a girl not having a father than a little boy."

"Oh, honey, you'll be a wonderful mother. Boy or girl, they'll never want for anything."

"I know. Still, it would be nice to have a father for my baby." For a moment Adam's face flashed into her mind. Amber shook her head as if to knock the image away. He had made it perfectly clear he was not interested in any pregnant woman. He probably hated children. And she was not interested in hooking up with any man at this point. She had lots more to do before she wanted to risk her heart again.

"Matt will be in high heaven if he gets to act as father to your baby. He can hardly wait for ours," Sara said.

"What a turnaround. You were afraid a few weeks ago

he'd leave when he learned you were pregnant. Now he's curtailed his traveling and knows more about babies than I do from all the books he's reading," Amber said in amazement.

"Once the idea took hold, he ran with it," Sara said, smiling serenely. "He's excited about the baby. I'm so glad." She jotted down the last measurement and looked up.

"Want to go out for something to eat? I'm craving a hot fudge sundae."

"I'll have one with you, then head home."

"No cravings?" Sara asked as they left the apartment.

Just seeing Adam run by and stop at the exercise bar, Amber thought, though she shook her head at her mother's question. She frowned. She was over that craving, after having met the man. At least she hoped she was.

When Amber returned to her apartment later, she spotted Virginia's car parked at the curb. Sighing, she entered the building. What did she have to do to have some privacy? This made the fifth day in a row Virginia had come by. She was no longer content with telephone calls.

Stepping into the elevator, Amber hesitated a moment, then in a gesture of rebellion, pressed the button for the rooftop. She'd sit on the deck a while and hope Virginia would get tired of waiting and leave.

Amber scanned the garden area when she arrived at the roof. There was that couple from the second floor. A student she recognized from campus looked asleep on a lounge chair. And Adam Carruthers, sitting near the edge, looking toward the ocean.

She walked over and sat in the chaise next to him. He glanced up, frowned and looked back to the ocean.

"How are you feeling today?" she asked.

"Hungry," he said.

She smiled. Maybe next time he'd learn not to snap at the hand that fed him. Though he'd had plenty of time to eat since dinner last night.

"So order in," she said, leaning back and gazing in the same direction. Sunshine sparkled on the water. The rays felt warm against her skin and she began to relax as she let the soft breeze cool her skin. Too bad there wasn't a larger apartment in her price range in this building. Then she wouldn't have to move.

"Mothers should be more compassionate," he mumbled halfheartedly. He was leaning back in the chair, his eyes narrowed against the sun's glare.

"I will be to my child," she replied. "But I'll also teach him to be polite so when someone feeds him he gets to finish the meal."

"How was I to know you're so touchy?"

"You could ask, how was I to know you would immediately leap to stupid conclusions."

He glanced at her. "You always bring your purse up to the roof?"

"No. My mother-in-law's car is out front. I thought I'd stop here first. Don't get me wrong, she's a lovely lady. But she's driving me crazy. First because of Jimmy, now because of the baby."

"Jimmy?"

"My husband." Amber felt Jimmy slipping further and further from her memory every day. She had pictures of him in the apartment, but when closing her eyes, she had trouble visualizing him. No trouble in remembering things they had done in high school or the plans they'd made. Just difficulty in remembering how his hair fell and the way his eyes looked into hers.

"You must really miss him."

"Not really." She opened her eyes and stared at him in dismay. "That didn't come out right. I do miss him. I can't believe I won't ever see him again. But for the last couple of years, he was stationed overseas, so we didn't have much to do with each other except e-mail. Then he was home for a few weeks, and now he's gone forever. It's so weird."

"Tell me about him," Adam suggested.

"Why?"

He shrugged. "Give you something to talk about and me something to listen to. I tried going to the fire station today, but the watch commander booted me out and told me not to show up again until I was ready to work. He means well, I know, but I'm bored with my own company."

"So hearing about a stranger you'll never meet is better than nothing?" she asked.

"Listening to your voice is what I'm after," he said.

"I'll read you a book." Amber was flattered by his implication.

"Tell me about Jimmy instead."

She complied, starting when they first met, what fun they'd had in high school, and how bummed she'd been when he enlisted.

"Sounds to me like he had some growing up to do."

"He was grown up. He was twenty-one."

"A great age."

"How old are you?"

"Twenty-seven. And from here twenty-one looks young."

"I'm only twenty."

"A baby," he teased.

She glared at him. "Not. I'm grown up. Soon I'll be a mother."

"Do you and the kid a favor. Give him up for adoption."

"What? Give up my baby? Are you nuts?"

"It's a hard life for a single parent. Much better for both of you to avoid the pitfalls before you become attached."

"Just because your childhood wasn't so great doesn't mean every child with a single parent can't have a terrific life. My mother was single almost my entire life. She went to school and raised me before getting a job. We had a great life."

"Where is she now?"

"Here in the city. She got married shortly after Jimmy and I married. I'm happy for her, but she wasn't searching for some man to take care of her like you said your mother was."

"My mother was the neediest woman I ever saw. She didn't seem to think she could do anything on her own, so she didn't. She complained about my father the entire time I was growing up. And tried to find a new father for me. Only it was really about someone for her. She was scared to be on her own."

"That's sad. I bet she did fine."

He was silent for a couple of moments. "You're right," he said with some surprise. "We had a clean apartment, never went hungry. It wasn't the life she wanted, though, and she never accepted what she had. She was always searching."

"Where is she now?"

"She died a couple of years ago."

"I'm sorry."

"Yeah, me, too."

"No siblings?" Amber asked.

He shook his head. "You?"

"I'm going to have a baby brother or sister in November."

"What?"

She nodded. "My mother is pregnant. She and Matt are thrilled. And her baby and mine are due practically the same day."

"You and your mother are pregnant? At the same time? How old is she?"

"She's thirty-eight. Matt's a few years younger. They're thrilled."

"What happened to your father?"

"He left when I was a baby. What happened to yours?"

"Same. Not named Carruthers, was he?"

"Nope, Simpson."

Adam fell silent, letting the quiet grow. Amber relaxed against the chair, almost dozing in the sun's warmth. She could stay up here the rest of the afternoon. And would, if Virginia didn't leave. When she had a bit more energy, she'd go to the railing to see if she could spot the car. Surely Virginia would get tired of waiting in the hall and leave.

"Want to get a pizza later?" Adam asked.

Amber was almost asleep. She rolled her head along the back of the chaise and looked at him through narrowed eyes. "I guess."

"I'll buy and we'll eat at my place. Then if you get in a snit, you can leave without finishing the meal."

She smiled sleepily and closed her eyes. "Sounds like a plan."

CHAPTER FOUR

ADAM looked at her. She was asleep. He glanced at her skin. It was not turning pink, but he'd keep an eye on the time. She didn't need to get sunburned.

He leaned back and tried to let go of the feeling he'd just done something stupid. How could he push her away with one hand and invite her to dinner with the other?

Looking at her again, as if unable to help himself, he knew the answer. She was better company than a rerun on television.

Heck, she was actually fun to be around. Prickly as all get out, maybe, but then he hadn't been at his best since accusing her of trying to trap him in marriage. At least he'd cleared that up. She wasn't looking for a man and he wasn't looking for a woman. Maybe they could muddle through until she moved. It beat being alone.

He didn't like to think how much of his life was wrapped up in his work. But being banned from the station sure made an impact. He'd call some of the guys tomorrow and see if they wanted to hang out on their day off. Three of the men on his shift were also single, though Bart had a steady girl. The other men and women were married, and always talking about family outings and obligations.

He liked being single. Being responsible for someone else's happiness seemed a burden too big to be borne. No wonder his father had left. Had Amber's father felt the same? Adam had more integrity than to desert someone who depended on him. Much better never to get entangled than to have to make a decision like that.

He nudged Amber's shoulder a little later. He was getting hot and wanted to get out of the sun. "I'm going inside. I think you should, too."

"Not if Virginia is still here," she mumbled.

"I'll check if you like."

She nodded sleepily.

He headed for the elevator. No one was left on the deck but Amber. The sun was low, but there were still several hours of daylight left. He'd make sure the way was clear and then see about ordering pizza.

The hall on her floor was empty. Did the older woman hound her? Maybe Amber should take a stronger stance and make sure Virginia got the message. He shook his head. From what he'd seen so far, Amber was too kind for her own good.

Reaching the rooftop in short order, he called across the expanse. "Coast clear."

She waved a hand but didn't sit up.

"You need to get out of the sun," Adam said, crossing the deck.

"I need to take a nap," she said grumpily.

"Downstairs, then." He pulled her up onto her feet almost laughing at the cranky look she gave him.

"Not if Virginia calls to see if I'm home."

"Nap on my bed, then. She can't call my place."

"Um."

Amber stumbled when she took a step. Adam put his un-injured arm around her waist and pulled her close against him. "No falling," he instructed.

Less than five minutes later he was in his apartment, a pretty blonde in his bed. Adam sat in the living room wondering what had possessed him to invite her to his bed. Now he would have a hard time not seeing her there when he went and used it himself.

He switched on the television, surfing until he found an old war movie. Not the greatest thing on the tube, but it was something to pass the time until his guest woke up and they could eat.

Amber awoke, disoriented as to where she was. The bed was huge, much bigger than her own single. The room was dark, shades pulled. The duvet on which she lay was as soft as a cloud. She ran her fingertips over the velvet cover. She remembered Adam letting her use his room so she didn't have to go home and be awakened by the phone if Virginia called.

Slowly she sat up. How late was it?

She went to the bathroom and splashed water on her face. She felt better for the nap. Heading to the living room, she stopped when she saw him sprawled on the sofa in the midst of some gun battle on TV.

"Sorry I slept so long," she said.

He looked over at her. "You obviously needed the rest."

She nodded. "I don't always sleep through the night. What are you watching?"

"It's almost over." He clicked it off. "A World War Two flick. I know how it ends."

She laughed.

"Ready for pizza? What do you want on it?"

They agreed on a pizza with everything and Adam called in the order. He poured them each a soda and sat beside Amber on the sofa.

She felt awkward. What would they talk about? Maybe eating dinner together was a bad idea. Yet she didn't want to return to her empty apartment. Pictures were already off the walls. Boxes had been packed and stacked near the door. The place looked bare and uninviting. Maybe she should begin moving her things into the other apartment. There was no reason to remain in this one until the end of her lease. She could move any time.

Looking at Adam, however, she decided there was no rush.

"If your mother-in-law is harassing you, maybe you need some deterrents," Adam said as he sipped his cola.

"She's not really harassing me," Amber said. Though when she thought about it for a moment, it almost seemed like it. "She's so excited about the baby. Jimmy was her only child, so she's latched on to the fact I'm having her grandchild. Learning that I was pregnant actually perked her up. She's been so depressed."

She wished she'd felt more depressed. She couldn't tell anyone except Bets how she felt. Her mother and Virginia would think she was crazy not to be grieving for months and months. But the truth was, she hadn't seen much of Jimmy since he'd graduated from high school two years earlier, and it was hard to miss someone who had been gone that long. Unless she thought about it, she could almost imagine he was still overseas.

"She needs something to take her mind off Jimmy and the new baby. If I let her, she'd have me moving into her home and letting her take over completely," Amber said.

"So tell her to bug off."

"I can't tell her that," she replied, horrified. "She's my mother-in-law."

"I'm not up on all the technicalities, but I think once your husband died, the relationships changed," Adam said.

"Still, she'll be one of the grandmothers of my child. I need to keep good relations going."

"I'm not saying cut her off at the pass, just set some boundaries. Otherwise, you're going to have to deal with this for a long time."

Amber didn't think she could set boundaries Virginia would accept. To the older woman, Amber was still that high-school girl who dated her son.

"What would you suggest?" she asked.

"Tell her not to call so often, not to show up unexpected. That's not asking too much," Adam said. He placed his glass on the table.

Amber held hers out to him. It was cold and she wasn't going to drink any more until the pizza arrived. His fingers brushed hers when he took it. She watched as he placed it on the coffee table beside his. The warmth from his touch seemed to linger. Maybe her hand had been colder than she thought. She felt that fluttery sensation in her stomach. She looked at him, swallowing hard as she tried to remember what they'd been talking about.

"I'll tell her, but she won't listen."

"Then you aren't being forceful enough. Tell her like you expect her to respect your wishes."

"You think I'm a wimp?" Amber suspected he was right, but it stung.

"Not necessarily. I hardly know you. But you seem nice to me. Maybe too nice."

Why was it *nice* seemed almost like an insult when Adam said it? She bristled. "I'm not too nice. There's nothing wrong in being kind to people who are hurting."

"But there is something wrong when you're sacrificing your own rights for someone else. If you don't want her to call, tell her."

"Great idea." She jumped to her feet.

"Where are you going?"

"To my place to tell Virginia not to call. And for practice, I'll tell you not to bother me again!"

She turned to leave but Adam caught her arm. Rising, he towered over her. Amber glared up at him. "Don't touch me!" she said.

Slowly his fingers released her, trailing over her skin as he held her gaze.

"I didn't mean now. Pizza's coming."

"Eat it all. I'm not hungry."

"Liar."

Her temper flared. "You don't know me. Leave me alone."

He held his hands out as if in surrender.

"I was offering some advice. Take what you paid for."

"Which was nothing."

"Then ignore it."

She turned and walked to the door. Adam followed her.

When she tried the handle, he placed his hand against the door and held it closed.

"Let me out," she said softly.

"Don't go," he replied.

She looked up. His eyes searched hers. Then he leaned forward and kissed her.

Amber stood stock-still in shock. His lips were warm

and firm, moving against hers in invitation. He didn't touch her anywhere except on the mouth, which was more than enough. She felt lightheaded. Slowly she leaned into the kiss, savoring the sensations that spread through her like melted butter. He made no further demands, didn't push for more, just let his lips caress hers while she thought she would float away in delight.

Her heart was pounding when he ended the kiss. He stayed close, his breath soughing across her cheeks. Slowly Amber opened her eyes.

"You can't kiss me," she said, trying to sound forceful. That wispy voice couldn't be hers. "I'm a widow."

"Which means you're free and available again."

"No it doesn't. I'm still mourning Jimmy."

"Doesn't matter. You're still free and available."

She stepped back, frowning. She had to get her thoughts under control, not fantasize about another kiss.

"I'm not free and available and even if I were, you are not someone I want to take up with."

"What's wrong with me?" Adam asked in surprise.

"First of all, you have a dangerous job. If I ever think about getting involved again, it won't be with someone who puts his life on the line every day."

"Every other day. I have alternate days off," he said smoothly, his eyes dancing in amusement.

"And I don't like arrogant men."

He raised an eyebrow.

"And I'm not interested in some man who doesn't want to commit."

The amusement left his face. He pushed back away from the door and headed for the center of the room. "So go."

Amber watched him close down. It was like seeing him

don a cloak or something. One minute he was warm and friendly, almost laughing at her, the next he was cold and remote—a different man.

She slipped out of the apartment and headed for her place feeling as if she'd had a lucky escape.

Reaching her door, she stopped. She'd left her purse in Adam's apartment. She was not going back up there!

But how to get inside her own place? She had given her key to one of her neighbors shortly after moving in—for emergencies. Crossing to the opposite door, she knocked, hoping they were home.

They were and in only moments, Amber was safely inside her own apartment.

The answering machine was blinking furiously when she looked at it. Reluctantly she played the messages.

The first two were from Virginia. Bets had called. Then Virginia again, growing more demanding in each message. Then her mother left a message.

"Amber? Virginia has been calling here all afternoon. When you get home, give her a call, will you? She's driving us crazy."

"Try being me, Mom," Amber said, erasing the message. Bets called again and yet another one from Virginia— this one almost hysterical.

Sighing softly, Amber dialed the number. Maybe she was too nice and let Virginia walk all over her, but she could understand the woman's grief, even if she didn't share the depth.

Maybe it was guilt that had her bending over backward to make things all right. She felt more guilt than grief. How dumb was that?

"Where have you been?" Virginia demanded when she

recognized Amber's voice. "We've been worried sick. I called, I stopped by. Really, Amber, I've been frantic. Your mother said you'd been over there earlier, but even she didn't know where you were."

"Virginia, I'm a grown woman. I don't have to answer to my mother or to you. I have a life, you know. What I do and with whom I do it are my own business, not yours or my mother's." Amber was surprised at her own words.

"I was worried about you," Virginia said stiffly.

"I appreciate that, but I'm fine. If anything awful happens, Mom is listed as the person to notify, so she would have known immediately. I really need to have some space. If you want to get together occasionally, let me know and we can work something out. But please don't keep stopping by."

"It's that man, isn't it?" Virginia said. "You're dating again."

"What man?" Amber said, trying to play dumb. Virginia wouldn't like hearing about Adam's role in Amber's sudden rebellion. Amber was surprised herself. Was this all in reaction to the word *nice*?

"The one you say is a neighbor."

"Adam? I'm not dating him or anyone else," Amber said firmly.

"Then I don't see why there is any problem."

"Nor do I, as long as we continue to respect each other's right to privacy. I don't drop by your place uninvited, and I would appreciate it if you would reciprocate."

"You are always welcome here," Virginia said.

"Thank you. Once I'm in my new apartment, I'll invite you and James for dinner."

"When are you moving? I thought it wasn't until the end of the month."

"That's right."

"So you don't want anything to do with me before then?" She sounded horrified.

"How about we talk on the phone a couple of times a week," Amber said, getting tired of holding firm. It would be easier to just give in and deal with her annoyance when Virginia pushed.

"Jimmy would be appalled at your attitude," Virginia said.

Amber wondered what Jimmy would have thought. He'd avoided both Amber and Virginia as much as possible when he'd last been home, in her opinion. The man could have done more to spend time with his mother, and her.

"Maybe, or maybe not. But that's the way I want it right now," Amber said, proud of the firm note in her voice.

"Hormones," Virginia said wisely.

"What?"

"Hormones affect pregnant women in various ways. You're going through a bad patch right now. I understand. I'll wait. Call me tomorrow."

She hung up before Amber could reply. Good grief, was it hormones? Was her every move and thought now influenced by the changes in her body with the baby?

A knock sounded on her door.

It couldn't be Virginia, she'd just hung up from talking with her. She crossed the room to open it. Adam stood there, her purse hanging from the hand that held the flat pizza box.

"Dinner," he said, stepping inside.

Immediately Amber felt as if the space had shrunk. Her apartment wasn't as large as his, but she'd never felt so crowded as she did now.

"I'm not hungry."

"Too bad, I ordered enough for two. You have to help

me eat it." He marched over to the small table that served as study center and dining area, and slipped the box onto the surface. He dangled her purse on his fingers.

"You forgot this."

She took the purse and tossed it on a nearby chair. The sooner he was fed, the sooner he'd leave. The aroma from the pizza box had her mouth watering. She loved pizza and it had been ages since she'd had one.

She drew out two soft drinks, glasses and two plates, then headed for the small table.

He held her chair for her and Amber felt that fluttery sensation again. Good manners were something her mother would love.

When they each had a slice of pizza, Amber began to eat hers without looking at him.

"Should I take my slices and head for home?" he asked a couple of minutes later.

She met his eyes. "Stay, you're already here."

"Rousing invitation. Maybe I'll take a page from Virginia's book."

"I spoke to her when I got home."

"A gazillion messages on the answering machine?" he guessed.

"A few. Anyway, I made it clear I didn't want her dropping by uninvited."

He looked around the apartment. "Working so far, I see."

Amber smiled. "So far."

The lighthearted comment defused the tension and Amber began to relax.

"You look ready to move," Adam said noting the boxes.

"I just about am. There's still all the kitchen stuff to pack up, but I don't have a lot, so I can just pack as I go."

"End of the month?"

"Maybe earlier if I can get the guys at my stepdad's work to help. They moved my mom and stepdad and it went great. Plus it was a lot of fun."

"If not, I can get some of the guys from the station to help out. We can do it on a weekday, when the traffic is less."

"Can't wait to get rid of me?" she asked, feeling just a twinge of disappointment at his offer.

"Not that. Just want to make sure I know where you're moving."

"I could give you an address."

He nodded.

The pizza was finished in short order. They lingered over the soft drinks, talking about many things.

When the rap came on the door, Amber looked up in surprise.

"Virginia," Adam guessed.

She groaned softly. "I told her not to come unless invited. I said I'd be in touch soon. Does she have to show up all the time?" She rose and headed for the door, the light of battle in her eye.

"Mom, Matt. I didn't expect you." Amber was startled to see her folks.

"Hi, honey," Sara said, stepping inside. "Virginia is in a hissy fit about you and we went out for ice cream and so..." She trailed off as she noticed Adam.

He'd risen when the Tuckers entered the apartment.

Sara glanced at the table with dinner clearly in evidence, back to Adam, then to Amber. "Are we interrupting?"

"Mom, Matt, this is Adam Carruthers. He has an apartment on the fifth floor. We were just sharing a pizza. Adam, this is my mother Sara and my new dad, Matt Tucker."

Adam shook hands with Matt. He smiled at Sara. "Nice to meet you."

"Nice to meet you," she replied with a quick glance at her daughter. "We won't stay. I just wanted to make sure Amber was okay."

"I'm fine. Come in and sit down. Did you get ice cream?"

"Your mother had a double hot fudge sundae. We can't keep the ingredients in the house, or she'd eat them three times a day," Matt said, teasing Sara.

"Or more. You're so lucky, you don't have any cravings," Sara said, sitting on the sofa.

Adam smiled and took a step toward the door. "I'll leave you all to visit," he said.

"Oh, no, you don't," Amber said, stepping between him and the door. "You can stay and visit. They said they wouldn't be here long."

"If we're intruding—" Matt said.

"No," Amber and Adam chorused together.

"How did you break your arm?" Sara asked when they were all seated.

If Amber had thought the apartment small when Adam arrived, it was positively minuscule now that she had another large male and her mother. At least the apartment she was moving to was big enough to have a few friends over at once without feeling they were stepping on each other's toes.

Adam had brought the chair from the dining table. Amber was perched on the edge of the end table while Sara and Matt shared the sofa. She hoped her mother wouldn't be staying long. But it would be too much to hope there wouldn't be questions soon as she got home.

"On the job. I'm a firefighter. Had a floor collapse on me a week or so ago and this is the result," Adam said, holding up his arm.

"A firefighter?" Sara asked. "That has to be one of the most dangerous jobs going."

"Not if you're trained for it. I've had excellent training."

"Still, the unexpected happens," Amber said, looking at his arm. She hadn't known the man for long, and wasn't even sure she liked him very much. But the thought of him plunging into a burning building sent shivers down her spine.

"Occasionally, but not as often as you might think. I've been doing this for seven years and this is the first major problem."

"You could have been killed."

"But I wasn't," Adam said gently.

She looked away.

Sara smiled brightly. "I have news," she said.

"What?"

"Matt and I are leaving for Athens next week!"

"Wow, Mom, that's fabulous. How long will you be gone?"

"A week at least," Matt said. He looked at Adam. "I'm a troubleshooter for my company, and we have a major problem with some clients in Athens. I've curtailed a lot of travel until after the baby is old enough to go with us, but when I mentioned this, Sara decided she was up for a week in Greece."

"I would be, too," Amber said.

"Do you travel a lot?" Adam asked.

"I used to. Now I'm home most of the time," Matt said.

"Only until the baby comes and gets old enough to

travel," Sara said, squeezing Matt's hand. "In the meantime, we do want to take a few trips."

"And you can, now that you finally quit your job," he said.

Amber felt a pang at the happiness the two of them shared. They complemented each other in ways she would never have expected. She was glad her mother had found happiness with a great guy like Matt. But deep down inside she was envious. She didn't have that special connection with anyone, not even with Jimmy when he'd been alive. She wished she could find that special something that made a couple perfect for one another.

"I was thinking of moving in a few days," Amber said. "Guess you two lucked out and won't have to help."

"Put it off until we return," Sara suggested.

"I'll see when the guys at work are available," Matt said.

"Actually Adam said he and some of his friends would help me," Amber said. "I think he wants to get rid of me."

CHAPTER FIVE

ADAM wanted to deny Amber's statement, but knew it would only add fuel to the speculative fire already burning in her mother. He rose and nodded to Amber.

"I'll be heading home. Let me know how soon I can get rid of you."

She jumped up and followed him to the door, and outside into the hallway, pulling the door almost shut behind her.

"Thank you for dinner," she said politely.

"Thanks for letting me in when I brought it down," he said gravely, wanting to laugh at her prim attitude. Instead, he did what he'd been wanting since about three hours ago, leaned over and kissed her again.

This one was not nearly as satisfying. It was too brief and too soon over. But he knew her parents were just on the other side of the door, and he didn't want to give rise to further speculation.

"I know," he said, tapping her chin with his finger, before she could say a word. "Don't do that, you're a widow. Ever hear of the merry widows, darling?"

With that he turned and headed for the stairs, not wanting to wait for the elevator.

He entered his apartment thinking about Amber. He felt

a touch of pride in her for standing up to her mother-in-law. Would she be able to hold to her edict?

Not that it mattered to him. She was just a soon-to-be-moving neighbor. They'd shared a pizza, no big deal.

But the kisses had been a big deal, he thought, flinging himself down on the sofa and switching on the television. He didn't watch it, however, his mind a million miles away, or one floor down.

Was her mother as pushy as Virginia? Would she demand answers Amber didn't want to give? Maybe he should have stayed longer, out-sat the parents and stayed by her until they'd gone.

That was a hell of an idea.

It was better to cool things. They'd eaten a couple of meals together. She'd be moving soon. He still had his bachelor life intact. No danger of falling for a pretty girl, especially one who was pregnant and had a mother-in-law who barged in at her own convenience. If she didn't cool things off, Amber would never find a man willing to marry her and take care of her and the baby.

Thinking about his own mother always made Adam feel helpless. He shook off the mood and began to channel-surf. There was bound to be something on that would take his mind off his pretty neighbor with the soft, warm lips.

"Well, that went well," Amber said to the empty room when her parents left. Sara had refrained from making a big to-do over Adam's being here. Matt had eyes only for Sara, so Amber didn't have to worry about him cross-examining her. But she waited for the other shoe to drop. Surely she wasn't going to be able to go to bed and get some rest without something else happening.

Sure enough, a half hour later the phone rang.

"Hey, girlfriend, what's up?" It was Bets. Amber clutched the phone with relief.

"I'm so glad it's you," she said.

"Who else would call you this late?" Bets asked.

"Virginia, my mother, who knows. Anyway, can you talk until midnight, I'm sure they'll all be in bed by then."

Bets laughed. "What's got the older generation in an uproar?"

"Adam."

"Whoa, who is Adam? Oh, wait, is he Adam of the body to die for that exercises in front of you every other day of the week?"

"He's a neighbor."

"What?"

Amber explained what had been happening over the last couple of days. Had it been such a short time since she found out Adam lived upstairs? She'd already shared two meals with him. And two kisses.

When she casually mentioned them, she thought Bets would come through the phone line.

"Tell all. I can't believe you've kissed the man. I thought you'd be a nun the rest of your life."

"Give me a break, Bets, Jimmy's only been dead a few months. I'm horrified."

"Honey, you are alive. It was only a kiss. What's the big deal?"

Amber didn't want to talk about it, didn't even want to think about what the big deal was. The fact she reacted to Adam's kisses more deeply than she had Jimmy's worried her. She and Jimmy had been high school sweethearts. She'd known she wanted to spend her life with him since she was sixteen. How could she even think about another man?

"Amber, you still there?" Bets asked.

"Yes. It isn't such a big deal, I guess."

"Unless you want more," Bets guessed.

"Of course not. A friendly kiss between neighbors, that's all it was. He offered to help me move. Obviously he can't wait to get rid of me."

"Hmm. When are you moving?"

"Soon."

"Include me in. I want to meet this Adam. Unless you want to have me over and invite him to dinner."

"Not likely. Let's change the subject. What have you been up to?"

Bets regaled her with tales of her weekend, which had been full of activities, and men. Amber didn't know how her friend had so many dates, and never seemed to settle on one particular man. Of course, that was a safe way to have fun and not get involved. No commitment for Bets until she had her degree! She'd said that more than once.

Amber had made her commitment—to Jimmy.

Until death do you part. The familiar condition echoed in her mind. Her commitment to Jimmy had been severed. As Adam said, she was free. But she was not available!

After Bets hung up, Amber was restless. She prepared some hot chamomile tea, and wandered around her small one-room apartment. Soon she'd be back in the place she'd called home most of her life. Things would settle down into some kind of routine. She planned to start school again in the fall, hoping she could work something out with her professors to take a leave for when the baby was born.

She had a lot to do before the child arrived. But she couldn't make up lists like Virginia liked to do. She didn't want to go shopping like her mother wanted.

She didn't know what she wanted.

Finally the soothing tea calmed her enough she could get to sleep.

The next few days Amber did her best to ignore her upstairs neighbor. She finished packing everything she didn't need on a daily basis. The boxes were stacked near the door. It wouldn't take much to move her across town—with a little help.

She ventured forth to the park a couple of times, making sure she chose a different time from the one Adam had normally used when exercising. She saw him one afternoon when she returned home. He was heading out and already greeting a friend who waited in a car.

Despite her best efforts to remain aloof, Amber strained to see who was driving. Some other guy. The relief startled her. She had no claim on Adam. If he wanted to date every day and twice on Sunday, fine with her.

He waved before climbing into the car. She lifted her hand, wishing wistfully that he was going to spend the afternoon with her.

When she reached her apartment, she called her mother.

"How are you doing?" Amber asked when Sara answered.

"I'm frantic with packing and trying to make sure all the deliveries will be covered and rescheduling appointments. I thought going to Greece was a good idea, but now I'm wondering."

"I can be at your place for deliveries, if you like," Amber offered. "Why didn't you ask me?"

"I know you're busy."

"Not really. In fact, I feel at loose ends."

"Oh, honey. Want to go with us?"

"No, Mom, I definitely do not want to go to Greece with you and Matt."

"Why not?"

"Talk about a fifth wheel. You know Matt hardly notices the rest of the world when you're around. You two go and have a great time. Let me know when I need to be at your place and I'll open the door for whoever."

"We're having the baby furniture delivered on Friday. We'll assemble the bed and all when we get back. If you wouldn't mind letting in the deliverymen."

"Of course not. What else?"

Amber jotted notes on things her mother was worried about, glad to have something to occupy herself in the next few days. Maybe she should take Adam up on his offer to help her move and get it over with. She could spend the time setting up her new apartment.

"That's everything," Sara said. "You'll be all right?"

"Of course. You two have a great time."

"How's Virginia?"

"So far, so good. She's called once a day, but hasn't come by. She blames my attitude on hormones."

Sara laughed.

"Who cares what she blames it on as long as she gives you some peace. You still seeing Adam?" she asked casually.

"I'm not *seeing* him. He's a neighbor. I saw him today as he was going out with a friend."

"I liked him."

"I like him, too. But it's too early to think about dating again," Amber said quickly. Was it because sometimes she did think about it?

"Not necessarily. Jimmy wouldn't want you to stay single."

"I guess. But I have so much going on with the baby and all, I don't have time to get interested in a new relationship. And how many men want to take on a ready-made family?"

"Lots of men, especially if it includes my wonderful daughter."

Amber shook her head, smiling. "Mom, you're prejudiced."

"Not about my kids. Wow, isn't that cool, kids? I can't wait!"

"Neither can I," Amber said. The reality felt strange, but she wanted to see her new brother or sister. Wanted to hold her own baby in her arms.

"Got to go. Thanks, sweetie, for taking care of everything for me."

"Just have fun," Amber said. She slowly hung up the phone, feeling a wave of sadness sweep over her.

Her mother sounded so happy. She had Matt, the exciting life they'd planned and soon a beloved child would complete their family. Amber knew she'd always be a part of her mother's life, but it wouldn't be the same anymore. Sara and Matt would have their own family. There was every likelihood her mother would have more than one baby. Amber would never live with her siblings, never get to know them on a day-to-day basis. She'd be more like an aunt.

Unexpectedly she burst into tears. She missed Jimmy.

Missed the life she had counted on sharing with him. She was afraid of having a baby all by herself. How would she manage? Should she consider Virginia's offer to raise her child?

She didn't want to do that. She wanted to love her baby, care for it and help it grow into a wonderful adult. She had so much she could share with a child. She'd tell him about his daddy every day.

Her tears came harder. How could Jimmy have died! It was so unfair. He'd been too young, he'd had a life to live, not to be cut short in some foreign country by some soldier he never even saw. She wanted her baby to know its daddy, to learn of that family and feel connected and whole. Not like a piece was missing—the way she felt not having any relatives beside her mother.

She didn't begrudge her mother her happiness, but it pointed out how alone Amber was, how lonely she'd be in the days and years to come.

Amber didn't know how long she cried. Her heart felt as if it were breaking. She struggled for composure, only to sob even harder. She had cried for days when she'd first learned of Jimmy's death. She should be beyond this. Yet, it wasn't only for Jimmy that she cried. She wept for herself.

"Amber?" A loud knock sounded on the door.

She sat up, holding her breath. She didn't want to see anyone. Especially Adam.

"Amber, open up. I can hear you in there. What's wrong?"

"Nothing. Go away."

"No." He knocked again. "Open up. I'm not going away."

She rose, blowing her nose and blotting her eyes once more. She opened the door and looked out at Adam.

"I'm fine. Go away."

He pushed the door open and stepped inside the apartment, reaching out to draw her into his arms.

"What's the matter, honey?" His voice was so warm and compassionate, she burst into tears again. It felt like heaven to be held against him, his good hand rubbing her back gently. She heard the door click shut but it didn't stop the crying. His voice was like a lifeline as she burrowed into his chest, trying to escape the sadness and hurt. He didn't say much, but the tone was reassuring, the words comforting.

Finally she felt spent. She rested her cheek against his chest, hearing the strong steady beat of his heart. His warmth surrounded her, his comforting touch eased the distress.

"What happened?" Adam asked.

"Nothing." She didn't want to raise her face, didn't want to have to look at him. She felt like an idiot. And was exhausted to boot. "It just caught up with me, I guess."

"What?"

"Being alone, having to raise this baby without its father. How happy my mother is."

"Isn't that a good thing?"

"Yes it is. I'm happy for her. But it does point out how unhappy I am."

"I didn't pick up on that," he said. He put his hands on her shoulders and gently pushed her away, bending down a little to look into her face. "You seem happy and doing great. I know you must miss your husband, but you've started to move on. Just take one day at a time."

She nodded.

"Go splash on some cold water and we'll go for a walk. Fresh air will do wonders," he said, gently pushing her toward the bathroom.

"You don't need to stay, I'm fine."

"I like someone with me on walks."

"You don't," she argued. "You exercised every day without anyone."

"That's different."

"I've been to the park today."

"Let's go to the beach."

Amber went to rinse her face in cool water, appalled at the blotchy skin, the swollen eyes. It was amazing Adam hadn't run like crazy after taking one look at her. Instead, he'd invited her to take a walk along the beach.

Ten minutes later she climbed into a small sports car, the top already down.

"My stepfather has a convertible sports car. I think my mom likes it better than Matt does," Amber said, fastening her seat belt. The sunshine was almost too bright to stand. She put on her dark glasses and watched as Adam backed the car from the narrow garage and headed the short distance to the edge of the Pacific.

They parked in a lot that held only a few other cars. Weekdays the beaches weren't crowded.

The breeze blew steadily off the water, fresh and cool. Crunching along on the sand, they headed for the damp area near the water. The breakers splashed up, near them, but they stayed just out of range of the surging water. When it receded, the damp sand glittered in the sun.

They walked in silence. The sound of the surf and the crying gulls made the perfect background. Amber began to relax, to feel rejuvenated being by the ocean. A few daring souls were swimming in the cold water, their shrieks and laughter carrying on the wind.

She stumbled and Adam's hand shot out, grasping her arm so she didn't fall. He slid his hand down to hold hers.

Amber felt his touch to her toes. Her heart slammed against her ribs, the tingling awareness that she always had around him notched up and filled her. She slipped her hand free. Too dangerous with the mood she was in.

"This is nice," she said, sidestepping just a bit to put some distance between them. "I love the ocean. My mother brought me often when I was a child."

"I like it, too. First time I came was when I moved to San Francisco about seven years ago. I spent my second day in the city walking along the beach, intrigued with all the water. Sometimes I wish we could harness it better to quench fires."

"A large hose directly from the sea," Amber said.

"Yeah, that'd be a hell of a way to put out flames."

"Your work is so dangerous," she said slowly, watching the waves break, relishing the feel of the fresh breeze.

"There is some danger, but it's dangerous to drive on the freeways. I've been trained, and I practice when the department does drills."

Amber shivered.

"Are you cold?" Adam asked, putting his arm around her shoulders.

"No. Just thinking we never know when life will end."

"Or begin. You and your mother are both on the brink of something exciting. Seems odd to know two generations will be doing the same thing, but your mother is young. And you'll have someone to share the ups and downs with."

Amber nodded, extremely conscious of his arm across her shoulders. For a moment she imagined they were lovers, strolling along the edge of the sea, sharing time and life together.

But they weren't lovers. And she didn't want to even think about such a thing. She needed to remember Jimmy. And remember, if she ever did fall in love again, she wanted her husband to have a safe job, not something dangerous like fighting fires.

"Do you ever fight the forest fires California has every year?"

"I went to the big one in L.A. a couple of years back. Normally our units aren't called."

"Walls of flames a hundred feet high," she quoted.

"I stayed clear of those."

Amber stopped and turned to face him, dislodging his arm. "Aren't you ever afraid?"

He shrugged slowly. "There's no time to be afraid when we are doing our job. Sometimes when it's all over, I think about what could have happened. But it didn't. We usually have a debriefing to go over what we did right, what went wrong, and how to combat such fires again. Keeps us on our toes, and our edge sharp."

"You weren't sharp enough to keep from falling through that floor and breaking your arm," she argued.

"The unexpected does happen. It's still the greatest job going."

"Are you an E.M.T.?" she asked, referring to the special Emergency Medical Technician training which went beyond mere first aid.

"I qualified a couple of years back," he said.

"But you still fight fires."

"If one of the regular E.M.T.s is out, I fill in. But, yeah, I'm usually fighting the fires."

She nodded and turned to start walking. She was clear in her mind. Even if she was interested in the man, there was no way she would risk her heart a second time with some man who flirted with danger on a daily basis. She'd move to her new apartment and forget all about Adam Carruthers.

Adam walked beside her, about a half step behind. He watched her, almost seeing the wheels turn in her mind. She didn't like his job. That was clear as glass. He felt defensive. It was a great job, one he was good at and liked. He was in line for a promotion soon. With any luck, in a few years, he'd be chief of a small station. Or he could join the arson squad, or move into full-time E.M.T. work. He had options and opportunities. But for the moment, he liked exactly what he did.

He hadn't considered how someone else would view his job. His mother had been more concerned that he make enough money to support himself. She had never voiced any concern about his safety. He always thought it was because she knew he'd been trained enough to stay as safe as anyone could. Or was it she hadn't thought it through, hadn't considered how dangerous it could be?

Glancing at Amber again, he wondered how to breach that wall. He wanted to see more of her. Since neither of them was in the market for a long-term relationship, what could it hurt to spend some time together?

"Given any thought to moving?" he asked. That didn't sound like spending time together. Dumb question.

"I'm ready to go, actually. If your offer is still good, I'd like some help. There's really no reason to stay where I am—except for the roof garden. I'll just have to get used to doing without."

"I'll ask some of the guys. Friday suit you?"

"Not Friday. I'll be at my mother's. They're expecting

the baby furniture to be delivered and I said I'd be there to let them in since they'll be in Athens."

"That's right, they're off to Greece."

Amber nodded, looking out across the expansive Pacific. She looked at her watch. "They're at the airport now. My mother loves to travel. Thanks to Matt's job, I bet she gets to see the entire world before long."

"How about you? Do you long to travel as well?" he asked.

Amber shook her head. "I might like to see some places sometime, but I'm happy staying right here. I've seen the snow in the Sierra in winter. Been to the hot southern California beaches. But mostly, I like staying close to home."

Adam shared her feelings, now that home was San Francisco. He had no burning urge to return to Fresno, where he'd been born and grew up. He loved the City by the Bay, however. When he first arrived, he'd explored all the various sections, from the Wharf to Chinatown, Japan Town and the Avenues. As a firefighter, he knew all the streets, and the quickest way to get from point A to point B. For relaxation, there were a plethora of activities, from swimming and surfing, to clubs and bars, to dancing or attending a rodeo.

Though he could relate to her loneliness. Sometimes it was hard to find someone to do things with. The guys were great, but most women he dated seemed to see it as a prelude to a deeper relationship. Those not husband hunting were few and far between.

They sat at one of the benches that faced the ocean.

"Thanks for suggesting we do this," Amber said.

He smiled but remained silent. She was always so polite. She'd make a good mother for her baby. It was a tough break that her husband died, but she had lots of support. Too bad his mother hadn't had it as well.

She cleared her throat. Adam glanced at her. Often that presaged an announcement that wouldn't be well received.

"I think we shouldn't see each other anymore, after I move. In fact," Amber continued, "you may not wish to help me move, if that's the case."

CHAPTER SIX

ADAM was caught by surprise. It was the last thing he'd expected to hear.

"The move comes with no strings," he said, touched a little by anger. "I'm not pushing this arrangement, though I did think we made the perfect couple. Neither is looking for a deep involvement, neither wants to marry. Who better to pal around with than someone who shares the same views?"

"I'm not palling around with anyone," she said stiffly.

"Figure of speech. Maybe not now, but in the future you might need an escort, or want to do something that would be more fun with two. If so, you can give me a call." Fine by him if she didn't want to hang around. He'd help her move to her new apartment, then let her make the next overture. If she really didn't want anything to do with him, so be it.

He rose. "Ready to head back? I don't want to impose my company on you any longer than necessary."

"Sit down," she said, looking up and reaching out to tug on his arm. "I didn't mean it like that. I just feel, I don't know, guilty, I guess. I shouldn't be going out with such a sexy guy when my own husband hasn't even been dead a year."

He sat. "A year? Is that the magic formula?"

"Usually people mourn for a year or longer."

"Usually?"

"I'm still mourning Jimmy. I wish he hadn't died."

"I wish the same thing and I never even knew the guy. To die so young is awful, no matter what the circumstances. But you didn't die with him. From what you said earlier, he's really been gone a lot longer than the few months he's been dead."

"Sometimes it feels as if I never knew him. He was so different when he was here in February."

"He wasn't part of your day-to-day life. There's not a wrenching hole he filled that is now empty. I bet you can still imagine him elsewhere in the world."

She looked at him in surprise. Adam wanted to wrap her in his arms and hold her. But he took a deep breath instead.

"That's exactly how I feel. How did you know?"

"That's how I felt when I heard my Mom had died. I was shocked, sad she was gone. But after the funeral and her affairs were settled, it didn't seem real. She lived in Fresno, I live here. I only saw her at Christmas, so her dying didn't change my day-to-day life significantly. Don't get me wrong. I loved her. I miss her. But sometimes I almost think she's at our place in Fresno, doing whatever it was she did after I moved out."

"So you don't think I'm too awful to feel that way?"

"I'd say it's perfectly normal."

She leaned back against the bench and seemed to relax.

Adam wished they taught grief counseling at the station. He didn't know much about it, except what he'd experienced when his mother died. In his book, Amber's feelings were expected. The guy hadn't been around, how could she grieve now when their parting had really taken place long before?

Amber wasn't sure how long they sat on the bench. She replayed the discussion, feeling relieved Adam didn't think badly of her because she wasn't as grief-stricken as Virginia was. Although her crying bout this afternoon had been due to grief. And fear. She would take one day at a time, as he said. Some days she'd be fine. On those when she couldn't hold it in, well, a good cry never hurt anyone.

"Want to go?" he asked.

"Yes. This has been great."

They headed back to the parking lot.

"Can we take a drive down the coast for a little way?" Amber asked when they reached the convertible. "Unless you have to get back for something."

"I'm not going back for anything. Tim took me shopping for lots of TV dinners that I can heat and eat."

"I'll cook dinner tonight, if you like. To say thanks for the beach trip," Amber said. Dinner wasn't seeing someone. It was just a way to say thank you for getting her out of the apartment and in a better frame of mind.

"You don't owe me anything," Adam said gruffly as he started the engine.

"I know, but I like to cook. And it'll save one of your dinners for later."

He gunned the engine and the car shot out of the parking lot like a bullet. They sped along The Great Highway, the Pacific on their right, houses flashing by on the left.

Amber loved it. The wind whipped through her hair, blowing it every which way, until she reached up to hold it away from her face. It was exhilarating! If she ever bought a car, she'd make sure it was a convertible. She felt carefree and happy as they drove miles down the coast.

An hour later they returned to Amber's apartment. She quickly washed up, pleased to see color in her cheeks, and that her eyes had lost the swelling.

"How about spaghetti," she asked when she came out to the kitchenette. "I can make garlic bread and a salad."

"Whatever, I like everything."

He sat at the small table and watched her as she went about preparing the meal. He offered to help, but she said no. With his arm, he should take things easy. Besides, Amber liked cooking, especially when it was for more than one.

"Do you cook?" she asked.

"As rarely as possible," Adam said.

"So you eat out all the time?"

"Not all the time. But more than you do, I bet."

"So learn to cook."

"Maybe I need a teacher."

She looked at him, a smile hovering around her mouth. "Is that a challenge?"

"Not if you don't plan to see me after you move."

The smile faded. "I think that's best."

"Why?"

She couldn't tell him it was to safeguard her heart. That she was attracted to him and didn't like the position that put her in. He'd probably laugh his head off after his comments earlier about neither of them being interested in an involved relationship. And how could she be interested and not want to see where it would lead?

She was better off sticking with her plan to cut him right out of her life.

"If you don't have a reason, then it's a dumb idea," Adam said.

"What?"

"I asked you why you didn't want to see me after your move and you don't have a single reason."

Caught. There was no way to explain.

The phone rang.

"Saved by the bell," he murmured.

She wrinkled her nose at him as she passed to pick up the phone.

"Amber?"

Her heart sank. It was Virginia.

"Hello, Virginia. What's up?"

"I'm calling to see how you're feeling. Better?"

Amber took a deep breath, trying to quell the instant annoyance she felt whenever she was around Virginia. "I'm feeling fine, Virginia. I'm not sick, I'm pregnant."

"I know, but hormones can wreak havoc with a woman's system. James and I want you to come for dinner Friday night. In fact, since your mother is out of town, maybe you should plan to stay the weekend with us. We can shop for some baby things."

"I have plans," Amber said desperately.

"What plans?"

Quickly she tried to think of something she could do that would satisfy the other woman. "My friend Bets and I are going to the show," she said.

"When?"

Amber's mind went blank. She looked at Adam. He was leaning back in the chair, balancing on the back two legs, watching her with that amusement that drove her crazy.

"Saturday. I'm not sure what time. Maybe afternoon, or evening."

"Well you can still come over afterward and stay the night. We can have a nice brunch on Sunday."

"On Sunday I'm... I'm..." Her look conveyed desperation.

Adam held up his arm and mouthed, *Visiting a sick friend.*

"...visiting a sick friend. Really, Virginia, I don't need to come to your house to stay for any length of time. It's not like I live that far away. Maybe you and I can have lunch one day next week."

"What day?"

"Tuesday," Amber said. "We'll meet at that place on Sansome that you like, at eleven."

The water was boiling, steam rising from the stove. Amber pointed to it. Adam looked over and rose, peering into the pan. He turned around and raised his shoulders.

Amber covered the receiver with her hand. "Put the spaghetti noodles into the pan, turn it down a bit and time it."

"Amber?" Virginia asked.

"Yes."

"Is someone there?"

"I have a friend over for dinner and I need to go. Dinner is almost ready."

"Who?" The sharpness in her tone once again annoyed Amber. She wasn't sure how she was going to handle Virginia over the next few years.

"A friend. I have to go. I'll see you on Tuesday."

Amber hung up even though she heard Virginia talking.

"You held tough," Adam said with admiration.

Amber went to check on the sauce. "It's hard, though. Virginia can be so needy."

"She has to find her own way. I know it's tough to lose a family member—I don't have anyone. But that doesn't make you hers."

"I know. She means well. I think she needs a new hobby. She was involved in some women's club, but when I asked her the other day about it, she blew it off. Doesn't have the same appeal, she said. She doesn't like to garden, to sew or anything as far as I can see."

"She'll dote on your child," Adam said.

"I hope not. I want a healthy relationship with the baby's grandparents, but not to be at their beck and call forever."

"She's scared," he said. "Once you marry someone else, she's afraid you'll forget about the baby's grandparents."

"I wouldn't."

"No, I don't think you would. But she does."

Amber hadn't thought about that. She frowned.

"I told you I didn't think I would get married again any time soon. Maybe never."

"Maybe, or maybe when the right guy comes along, you'll fall hard and fast."

She laughed. "Don't see it. How about you?"

"Never marrying."

"Unless the right woman comes along and you fall hard and fast," she repeated.

"I'm having too much fun now," he said, leaning over to kiss her.

Steam filled the small kitchenette area. The soft bubbling of the water provided a soothing background noise. Amber felt Adam's touch to her toes. She leaned against him, savoring the feeling of his arms coming around her, holding her, sheltering her. His mouth wrought miracles. Her being focused on the sensations that coursed through her as he moved his lips against hers, drawing a response she was more than happy to give. Endless moments drifted by until the sound of water splashing on the stove burner penetrated.

She pulled away. The spaghetti water was bubbling over the edge of the pot.

She quickly turned down the heat and pulled the pan away. In a moment, she slipped it back onto the burner. "Glad it was only water," she said, keeping her gaze firmly on the food cooking on the stove. "If the sauce had bubbled over, it would take me forever to get it cleaned up."

He moved away, giving her much-needed breathing space. Her heart pounded. Her mouth still craved his touch. She wasn't interested in eating dinner, she wanted to feel his arms around her again, savor the taste and touch of him.

"Dinner is almost ready," she said.

Adam didn't care a fig for dinner. He studied Amber. She avoided looking at him. He didn't blame her. She probably wanted him to leave and was too polite to say anything. He had no business kissing her. She was vulnerable. He should stand her friend, or get out. Not latch on to her like she was the best thing that ever happened to him.

He scowled and walked the few steps to the center of her small apartment. He couldn't even work up a good pacing here. Not that he needed to pace. They'd eat dinner, behave civilly and then he'd leave.

Only—he glanced out the window, almost afraid to give thought to his feelings—only he didn't want to leave. He wanted to spend some more time with Amber. Find out more about her. Learn what she liked to do when she wasn't studying to be a schoolteacher.

Discover how she planned to make room in her life for a baby and keep to her goal of becoming a teacher.

"It's ready," she said.

Adam turned and went to the table. She'd already served their plates, and placed the salad and hot garlic bread in the center. He held her chair. She smiled at him over her shoulder. At least his mother had taught him manners. Which Amber seemed to like.

Seated a moment later, he was pleased to note she met his look full on, no averting her eyes.

The first bite exploded with flavor. "This is terrific," he said. "You said you liked to cook. If I could cook like this every day, I'd like to cook, too."

She smiled at his compliment. "Thanks. I don't cook like this for one. Usually I eat my main meal at lunch, on campus. Then just have sandwiches or soup for dinner. I thought firefighters took turns preparing meals."

"We do. But the crew made sure I only get lunch— which is sandwiches. I guess they figure I can't mess up on those too much."

The tension from the kiss seemed to have dissipated. Gradually he relaxed and enjoyed the meal.

Despite wanting to stay, once the dishes were washed and put away, Adam announced his departure.

Amber didn't try to change his mind.

"Thanks for taking me to the beach," she said, walking him to the door. "I'm sorry I cried all over you."

"Any time." He stopped at the door feeling like an uncertain teenager again. Did he kiss her, or just pat her shoulder and leave? Would she let him kiss her again? Or

had she had it with him trying to come on to her? She was
so into that widow role, he wasn't sure he wasn't pushing
just to get a reaction.

Wrong. He was pushing because he wanted her.

"Good night," Amber said, holding the door open.

He pushed it shut and drew her into his arms. Her eyes
widened slightly, but he was sure he saw a spark of happiness before she closed them to his kiss.

Adam was going crazy with boredom. His arm was feeling better. It no longer ached all the time. He hoped it was
healing fast so he could get back to work. This forced inactivity was driving him nuts.

It had been two days since he'd seen Amber. He wanted
to call her, but didn't have her number. He'd checked the
listings in the phone book, but there was no A. or Amber
Woodworth. He couldn't remember her maiden name,
which was probably what the phone was listed under.

He'd walked downstairs twice but didn't stop, turning
around and retracing his steps. She knew where he lived.
She could make some effort if she wanted to see him.

That was the kicker. He didn't think she did. Not as
much as he wanted to see her.

Thursday he spent the day cleaning the apartment, doing
laundry, stopping at her floor on his way down and back
to the laundry room. Never saw another soul.

Friday Adam decided enough was enough. He'd risk another visit to the station to do something, if only to sit and
watch while the on-duty crew washed the rig.

He was almost ready to leave when his phone rang.

"Adam, I'm running so late. I overslept. Can you possibly give me a ride to my mom's apartment?" Amber's

frantic voice came through almost in a jumble, she was talking so fast. "I'm supposed to be there when they deliver the baby furniture this morning and I can't make it on time going on the bus."

"Calm down. Of course I can give you a ride. Are you ready?"

"I will be in five minutes. Thank you, I owe you." She hung up.

He smiled. He liked the thought of her owing him. What would equal a ride to her mom's place? Dinner every night for a week? The thought had possibilities.

Amber gave him directions when they were in his car a few minutes later.

"Sorry if I'm keeping you from something," she said, almost straining against the seat belt in her effort to go faster.

"Nothing important. Relax. We'll get there when we get there."

"I know." She checked her watch. "It's not quite nine. They said they'd be there between nine and noon."

"I've never known delivery people to show up until the last moment. Which always makes me wonder how many people they really have deliveries for. Somewhere in the scheme of things, I should be first on the delivery list, wouldn't you think?"

Amber laughed. Adam caught his breath. He loved hearing her laugh. He chanced a glance and had a hard time returning his gaze to the road. She was beautiful when she laughed. He wished he could hear it every day.

"It's on this street, up about three blocks," Amber said when he turned onto the street near the marina. "Oh, look, the truck is in front. Quick, don't let them drive away."

Adam saw a man walking up the three stairs to the lobby when he pulled in behind the double-parked truck. If traffic had to go around the truck, it could go around him.

Amber scrambled out and hurried to the man on the stairs. Adam watched as they talked for a moment, then Amber nodded. She came back to the car.

"They just got here. Thank you for the ride. I made it!"

"I'll park and come help. Then I can give you a ride home," he said.

"You don't need to," she said. "I know you have things to do."

"It'll keep. I'll be back as soon as I find a parking place."

Fortune favors the few, he thought a moment later as he turned the corner and saw an empty parking place at the curb. He slid in, amazed at how easy it was. In only seconds he was back at the apartment building. The lobby door had been propped open so he stepped inside. He hadn't a clue where Amber's mother and stepfather lived. He'd have to wait for the delivery men.

He rode up with them on their next load, following them into the large apartment which overlooked the Bay. The living room was about the size of his entire apartment. The floor to ceiling windows had minimal coverings, framing the spectacular view.

Pausing only a moment, he continued down a short hall to the bedroom designated for the new baby. A new changing/dresser was against one wall. Several large boxes were leaning against another wall. A border of bunnies and teddy bears had been placed at shoulder level around the room. Curtains on the windows matched.

"That's it, sign here," one of the men was saying, holding out a clipboard with papers for Amber's signature.

Amber signed and thanked the men. When they'd left, she looked at the boxes.

"I thought all the furniture would come assembled."

"Too bulky that way," Adam said. "Want to assemble the pieces for your mother?"

Amber couldn't believe Adam had offered to assemble the crib and rocker. Didn't he have something else to do today besides help with another family's furniture?

Yet, how cool to have it all set up when her mother returned. She knew where the crib sheets and blankets were already stored.

"If you wouldn't mind, that would be great. Then when they get home, the room will practically be complete."

"I don't mind. I have some tools in my trunk, unless you know where Matt keeps his."

"I don't. And I'd feel a bit funny going through all their things looking for them. It was one thing when Mom and I lived in our apartment. I grew up there, I already knew where everything was. But this—it's not really my home anymore."

"I'll get what I need and be right back."

Less than a half hour later, the parts of the crib were spread over the floor in the baby's room and Amber was handing pieces to Adam when he requested them. He studied the directions for assembly for a moment, then put the paper aside. From there on, it seemed as if he knew instinctively how to put together a crib.

She watched fascinated as the bed took shape. Even the cast on his arm didn't hinder his efficiency.

"Have you done this before?" she asked.

He looked up. "What, put together a crib?"

"Yes."

"Maybe once. But I've done other projects. We do work in various communities as part of our outreach at the fire station. Once on vacation, I went on a Habitat for Humanity project in Arizona. Hot as could be, but rewarding work. Especially when the family saw their new home for the first time."

"Tell me," she said, sitting beside him on the rug. There was more to this man than she suspected. She'd known him for weeks, and yet hardly knew him at all.

As the morning progressed, Adam regaled her with his forays into construction and assembling toys for children at Christmas as he assembled first the crib, then the glider-rocker her mother had ordered. His funny stories didn't jive with the efficient, knowledgeable manner in which he assembled the furnishings. She suspected he was elaborating for her enjoyment. And she was enjoying herself.

Twice she laughed aloud at his tales.

"You're outrageous, that couldn't have happened," she said at one point.

He looked up, the familiar amusement dancing in his dark eyes. "I said so, didn't I?"

It was after noon when he gave the glider-rocker a push. "Try it," he suggested.

Amber sat in the chair, moving gently, as if rocking. "This is great. I guess I'll get one after all. I thought I wanted a traditional rocking chair, but this is so smooth and easy to rock on."

He pushed the crib against the long wall. "I don't know where they want everything," he said, gathering up his tools.

"Me, either. It looks good there. Wait a minute. I want

to make the bed and put in a couple of the stuffed animals they've acquired."

In moments the bedroom looked ready for its new occupant.

Amber stood in the doorway and looked at it all. Would her own baby's room be as nice? Probably, since her mom and Matt were insisting on buying the furnishings. Of course, that second bedroom at the old apartment wasn't as large as this one. But she did cozy just fine.

Adam put his arm around her shoulder and looked at the room.

"It's nice, isn't it?" she asked, leaning slightly against him. For a split second she could almost imagine Adam was the father of her baby, and they were admiring the room they'd prepared for their child.

Quickly she moved away. Foolishness, nothing more.

"Thank you for doing all this." She waved her hand indicating the room. "It'll be a great surprise when they come home."

"I enjoyed it. Let's get rid of all the boxes and then we'll be ready for lunch."

"Oh, um, I, uh, have plans," Amber said, caught by surprise.

"What?" he asked, looking directly at her. "Can't be visiting your sick friend, that's on Sunday."

She felt the heat rise in her face. She didn't lie worth beans.

"I'm happy to take you to lunch if you like," she said. The wiser move would be to flee from the attraction that plagued her whenever she was around Adam, or thought about him, or dreamed about him. But she did owe him for the ride, and for helping her assemble everything.

"I thought we could eat lunch at Embarcadero Center,

An Important Message from the Editors

Dear Reader,

If you'd enjoy reading romance novels with larger print that's easier on your eyes, let us send you TWO FREE HARLEQUIN ROMANCE® NOVELS in our LARGER-PRINT EDITION. These books are complete and unabridged, but the type is set about 25% bigger to make it easier to read. Look inside for an actual-size sample.

By the way, you'll also get a surprise gift with your two free books!

Pam Powers

Peel off Seal and Place Inside...

FREE BOOKS
LARGER-PRINT EDITION

See the
larger-print
difference.

THE RIGHT WOMAN

she'd thought she was fine. It took Daniel's words and Brooke's question to make her realize she was far from a full recovery.

She'd made a start with her sister's help and she intended to go forward now. Sarah felt as if she'd been living in a darkened room and someone had suddenly opened a door, letting in the fresh air and sunshine. She could feel its warmth slowly seeping into the coldest part of her. The feeling was liberating. She realized it was only a small step and she had a long way to go, but she was ready to face life again with Serena and her family behind her.

All too soon, they were saying goodbye and Sarah experienced a moment of sadness for all the years she and Serena had missed. But they had each other now and that's what

She held

Like what you see?
Then send for TWO FREE
larger-print books!

Printed in the U.S.A.
Publisher acknowledges the copyright holder of the excerpt from this individual work as follows:
THE RIGHT WOMAN Copyright © 2004 by Linda Warren. All rights reserved.
® and TM are trademarks owned and used by the trademark owner and/or its licensee.

YOURS FREE!
You'll get a great mystery gift with your two free larger-print books!

The Harlequin Reader Service™ — Here's How It Works:

Accepting your 2 free Harlequin Romance® larger-print books and gift places you under no obligation to buy anything. You may keep the books and gift and return the shipping statement marked "cancel." If you do not cancel, about a month later we'll send you 4 additional Harlequin Romance larger-print books and bill you just $3.82 each in the U.S., or $4.30 each in Canada, plus 25¢ shipping & handling per book and applicable taxes if any.* That's the complete price and — compared to cover prices of $4.50 each in the U.S. and $5.24 each in Canada — it's quite a bargain! You may cancel at any time, but if you choose to continue, every month we'll send you 4 more books, which you may either purchase at the discount price or return to us and cancel your subscription.

*Terms and prices subject to change without notice. Sales tax applicable in N.Y. Canadian residents will be charged applicable provincial taxes and GST.

If offer card is missing write to: Harlequin Reader Service, 3010 Walden Ave., P.O. Box 1867, Buffalo, NY 14240-1867 then go over to the baby store and check out your own furniture. Unless you already know what you want," he said.

Amber's heart sped up again. He was willing to go *baby shopping*?

"I haven't decided. But Mom and I measured the space a little while ago, so I know what I can and can't get. My baby's room won't be this large," she said, glancing around again.

"Babies aren't too big, they don't need a lot of room," he said. "Lunch?"

"Fine, thank you. But I'll treat, I owe you."

He lifted the tool box and a couple of the larger folded cardboard pieces and headed for the front door. "I'll treat. I'd rather you cook me a few more meals before you leave, if you really feel you owe me."

"That's too easy," she said, picking up several pieces and following him.

They locked the apartment, deposited the cardboard in the apartment Dumpster and headed for his car, lunch and shopping.

Amber was tired when they reached home. And feeling fairly guilty once again. She wondered if that would be a constant feeling. Guilt that she was alive and Jimmy was dead. Guilt she enjoyed herself today, instead of being in tears as she had been earlier in the week. Guilt she shared her choice of furniture first with Adam instead of her mother or Virginia. Guilt they'd bought the baby's first teddy bear together. Along with a few other items. She protested she'd only have to move everything, but Adam insisted.

Guilt was something she was getting used to, she thought as they waited for the elevator. Would it fade? Or was it something that would be with her for as long as she lived?

The elevator stopped on her floor and they both stepped out.

"Where have you been?" Virginia asked.

CHAPTER SEVEN

AMBER tried to smile politely, but a spurt of anger flared instead. "What are you doing here?" she asked. She'd told Virginia they'd get together next week. The woman had no business showing up unannounced. Hadn't Amber made that clear yet?

Virginia stared at Adam. "He's the reason you don't want me over here. What is going on? Jimmy would be horrified. What are you doing? You forget him so quickly, on to the next man?"

Amber was so surprised by her words she couldn't respond. Was that what everyone would think? That she didn't care Jimmy was gone? That she couldn't wait to get back on the dating scene again? It wasn't true!

"I don't believe we've been introduced," Adam said, filling in the gaping silence. "I'm Adam Carruthers, a neighbor from upstairs." He held up the bags from the baby store. "I was helping Amber carry up the bags."

It could sound as if he'd just met her in the lobby, Amber thought. Not that she was trying to hide anything.

Virginia didn't look mollified.

Amber stepped around her and unlocked her door. Thank goodness she'd never given Virginia or James a key.

She didn't know what had happened to Jimmy's, but at least his mother didn't have it.

Adam handed the bags to Virginia and left. Amber was torn between wishing he'd stood by her, and feeling glad he'd gone in case his presence agitated her former mother-in-law.

Amber waited until Virginia came inside the apartment and closed the door before speaking.

"I am so angry I can hardly stand it. I asked you not to come over here unless invited. You've embarrassed me in front of a neighbor, and you are driving me crazy. Virginia, I do not want you hounding me like this! I have my own life to lead and I need my space to do that."

"You're Jimmy's wife, the mother of my grandchild—" she started.

"I'm now Jimmy's widow. You will always be the grandmother of my baby, but the baby isn't born yet. I am in perfect health, so there is no need to worry on that account."

"You are all the family we have left," Virginia said.

Amber's heart ached for the woman. Her baby hadn't even been born, yet she was bonding with the child that grew beneath her heart. How would a mother stand losing her precious child? She sympathized with Jimmy's mother. But she couldn't let that sympathy establish patterns that were driving her crazy.

"I will always hold you and James in the highest regard," she said slowly. She gave the woman a hug, wondering if she'd made a mistake when Virginia clung.

"But I am not your child. Jimmy was. I have a mother and now a new stepfather. Virginia, I can't be your daughter. I can't take Jimmy's place," Amber said firmly.

The older woman released her and went to sit on the

sofa. She had tears in her eyes. "I only want what's best for you and Jimmy's baby."

"I know you do. I appreciate—"

A knock sounded on the door. Amber spun around and went to see who was there, wondering if Adam had come back to offer moral support.

A young man in a crisp Army uniform stood at attention before her.

"Mrs. James Woodworth?" he asked, not making eye contact.

"Yes?"

He relaxed a smidgeon and looked at her. "Jimmy's wife?"

She nodded.

"I'm Lance Corporal William Collins. I was with Jimmy when he died. He asked me to give you a message."

"Come in." Amber held the door wide, her heart racing. This man had been with Jimmy at the end. She had been told there had been only one survivor from the attack. When he stepped inside, she made the introductions. "Do have a seat," she urged.

He sat stiffly on a chair while Amber sat beside Virginia on the sofa.

"You were with Jimmy at the end?" she prompted.

He nodded. "Sorry to be so long in getting here, but I just got out of the hospital in Bethesda yesterday."

"You were injured in the attack," she guessed.

"Yes, ma'am. I was the only survivor."

"How fortunate you were. I'm sorry you were in the hospital for so long. Are you all right now?" Amber stared at him, seeing some of the man Jimmy had been when she'd last seen him. Young, full of pride in the work he did. A little distant and focused on other matters.

"I'm on my way home for convalescent leave. I hope to rejoin my unit in a few weeks," he said.

She took a deep breath. This young man had escaped death when all the others in the vehicle had been killed. Yet he was planning to jump back into the fray at the first opportunity. She didn't understand men at all.

"Jimmy was my son," Virginia said needlessly. Amber had introduced her as Jimmy's mother.

"Yes, ma'am." He looked at Amber. "He didn't suffer. We were hit without warning. The driver and Gary, the other man riding on the left side, were killed instantly. Jimmy and I were thrown from the vehicle, landing a few feet from each other. I crawled over to try to help. There wasn't anything I could do."

He seemed as distressed as Amber felt. Her heart went out to him. He would have to live with that regret forever.

"I'm sure you did your best, thank you," she said gently.

Virginia gave a small sob.

"He wasn't in any pain, ma'am. He said he felt numb from the neck down. He didn't live for long, but he wasn't in any pain."

Amber nodded, wishing she could have been there with Jimmy. Knowing this man had tried to help made all the difference in the world. She knew nothing could have saved her husband, but it was comforting to hear he had not suffered, nor been alone at the end.

"His last words were about you. He told me to tell you. Made me promise. I would have come anyway. But I gave my word."

Amber nodded, feeling the overwhelming sadness take hold.

"He said, 'I wish I could see her smile again. She has the best smile in the whole world. It lights up her whole face. Or hear her laugh. It's magical, making everyone smile who hears it.'"

Amber blinked back tears, almost hearing Jimmy's voice.

The young soldier cleared his throat, and glanced down at the beret he was twisting in his hands. "He said he wished he could kiss you just one more time."

The tears welled.

"Then he said, tell her I love her best." He looked at her, then at Virginia.

Virginia was in tears as well.

Amber tried to stem the tears, but they kept falling. "That was a joke between us. One of us would tell the other we loved them, then the other would say, I love you more. We went back and forth until finally one of us would say, I love you best. Then we'd kiss."

She'd never again be able to tell Jimmy how much she loved him. She would never again have another one of his kisses, laugh with him in the sunshine. He had had the last word.

The young man cleared his throat again. "Then he said, 'Tell her to find a great guy and have a huge family and name one of the kids for me. I want her to be happy, not be tied up with old memories. Tell her to live long, live happy and think of me once in a while.' Then he died."

Amber burst into tears, trying to stop crying, but feeling the ache in her heart as never before. Even when dying, Jimmy had thought about her. And about her future. He'd given her his blessing on whatever she decided to do.

A weight lifted from her shoulders. The sadness would

pass in time. And she would go on, with their child. She wished he'd known he was going to leave a child behind.

"Thank you for coming," Amber said, wiping the tears from her cheeks, wishing she had a tissue or something. "Thank you for being with him when he died so he didn't die alone."

"I wouldn't have left him, ma'am."

"I know you wouldn't. How long before help arrived?" she asked.

"A couple of hours later," he said, looking down at his hands, still gripping his beret.

Her heart ached anew. He must have been so scared, wondering if help would come in time for him with all his comrades dead around him.

"I'm glad you're all right," she said gently.

Virginia had found a handkerchief in her pocketbook and was dabbing her own cheeks. "I second that," she said. "I'm glad to know he didn't suffer and wasn't alone at the end."

"He's buried in Colma, in the National Cemetery there," Amber said.

"Good to know. I'd like to visit the grave my next trip here. But not this time."

"I understand." She brushed the tears away again. Sometimes she felt as if she'd spent the last several months of her life crying. Yet Jimmy's final words opened the gates to the future. He had wanted her to move on. She would do so without the guilt that has so plagued her.

"Anything else I could tell you?" Will asked.

"Don't go just yet," Amber said. "I'll fix us something to drink and you can tell us about Jimmy and his work over there—what you can, of course. Was he happy for the most part?"

"He loved working in communications. We have the latest in satellite uplinks, in observance equipment and telecommunications. He learned a lot, was up for promotion after that assignment. He and I worked together for several months." Will seemed relieved to have fulfilled his promise. He relaxed and began to tell Amber and Virginia about life on the Army post overseas.

Lance Corporal William Collins stayed for more than an hour, sharing stories about their adventures in Europe, and then the temporary assignment in a dangerous spot that ended so tragically.

He left when time grew short for his flight to Seattle. Virginia left a few moments later.

Amber cleaned the cups and put them away, thinking about all Will had told them. Jimmy's words echoed over and over in her head. She wished so much things had been different, but they were as they were. He'd known the end was near, and had given her his blessing to move on.

Maybe he had loved her best.

Saturday morning Amber slept in late, having the first good night's rest in a long time. Bets was due to arrive at eleven. They were going to lunch and the cinema just as she'd told Virginia. Amber couldn't wait to tell her friend what had happened.

She wanted to tell Adam, too, but hesitated. Theirs was a tenuous relationship. Both said they didn't want a relationship, yet she was growing involved. Look at her inclination to immediately share the information Will had given.

For a moment, she wondered if Adam would see her telling him as a subtle hint to let him know she was ready to find a new relationship and become a couple again. He'd feel threatened, she knew.

Maybe she shouldn't tell him. Maybe she should move to the old apartment, and ease off any contact with the man. He didn't want a future together.

But she was beginning to have doubts about her own protestations.

She liked being with him. He made her feel safe and cherished. She knew he was a man to depend upon. Too bad he had such a dangerous job, not to mention such a biased view toward pregnant widows.

Better she continue as they had been.

"Hey, girlfriend," Bets said breezily when she sailed into the apartment right at eleven. She gave Amber a quick hug and then studied her for a moment.

"Looking bigger than the last time I saw you. Clothes getting a bit snug?"

"I'm into elastic waist pants now, can't close my jeans. But I like my bigger breasts, I actually have a cleavage. Not that anyone's seeing it to be impressed."

Bets laughed. "Let's pick up a couple of low cut tops and see if cleavage has any effect on your neighbor. Will he be dropping by sometime?" she asked.

"Not likely. You ready to go? I don't want too big a lunch, I like popcorn at the movies."

The two young women left, talking and laughing. They took the bus to the mall where there were shops, fast-food restaurants, and a multiscreen theater. On the ride, Amber told Bets about Will Collins' visit.

"Wow, that's so cool. He came all the way to give you Jimmy's last words. Wish I could have met him."

"You want to meet every male in sight," Amber said.

"No, really, he sounds special. That was really a great thing he did. Right out of the hospital, too. How do you feel about it? I mean, it had to be tough hearing Jimmy's last words, but don't you think he gave you his blessing to go forward?"

"It sounded like it to me. But not yet, I'm sure."

"Oh, he had a date tagged on? I hope you have a happy life starting in four years, seven months and thirteen days, or something?"

Amber smiled and shook her head. "No dates attached. But I'm not ready."

"What about Adam Carruthers?"

"He's just a neighbor. Besides he's a firefighter. The last thing I'd want to do is fall for some guy who has a dangerous job. What if after a month of marriage, he got killed? I don't think that's a pattern I want repeated."

"I don't know, there are a lot of older firefighters. Plus they move up in the ranks and have easier jobs than the front line."

"Still, I think I want another teacher, or an insurance agent or something."

"Boooorrrring," Bets said. "I want someone with dash and flair."

Amber knew Adam would fit that bill. She should introduce the two of them.

The thought didn't sit well.

Maybe later, after she moved, she'd see about introducing them.

The day spent with her friend was fun. Bets had an irreverent way of looking at things. Her upbeat optimistic personality seemed contagious and by the time Amber returned home in the early evening, she was feeling better than she had in months. She hadn't laughed so much in ages. They agreed to get together more often over the remainder of the summer, and talk every few days on the phone. Bets worked full-time during the summer to afford school. But there were plenty of weekends and evenings.

Amber felt restless when she was alone. She went up on the rooftop deck to sit and watch the sunset. The couple from the third floor was there, with eyes only for each other. She wanted to tell them to cherish every moment together, but no one felt life would end soon, and they'd probably think she was crazy.

She pulled a chair near the rail and sat. Putting up her feet, she rested her hands on her tummy. She could feel the baby move from time to time, like a little flutter of a butterfly. She and her mother had discussed the changes, and how they felt about carrying new life—awestruck and humble, and thrilled beyond belief. Amber loved this child. How blessed she was to have it.

"Care for company?" Adam asked, standing near her.

"Sure do." She flashed him a smile, wondering if he thought it lit her face like Jimmy had.

"What did you do all day?" he asked after he dragged another chair over and sat. They were far enough from the other couple their conversation wouldn't be overheard.

"Went to the show with my friend Bets. We saw a comedy and laughed ourselves silly."

"Your mother-in-law okay?" he asked.

She nodded and looked at him speculatively.

"What? Do I have mustard on my chin or something?"

Amber laughed. "No, I was just thinking about something. After you left yesterday, I had a visitor." She proceeded to tell him about Lance Corporal William Collins, and the message he delivered. Adam listened attentively.

"How did you feel, hearing from your husband after so long?" he asked.

"It felt totally strange. And sad. And yet, I'm so glad to know he wasn't alone, that he didn't suffer pain. I felt sorry for Will. Imagine how he must have felt after Jimmy died."

Adam nodded and gazed out toward the ocean. "Tough position to be in. Nice of him to come by."

"It wouldn't have been the same in a letter, he said."

"Probably not."

Amber wasn't sure what she expected, but it was not this seeming disinterest. Not knowing what to say, she kept silent.

The sun was low on the horizon. Before long it would slip beneath the edge and darkness would fall. If he didn't say something by then, she'd get up and leave.

Adam looked at her again. "You okay with all this?"

"I'm fine. Why wouldn't I be?"

"Seems to me it brings it all back, like it just happened, instead of happening several months ago."

Amber nodded. "In a way. But the best part was where he said go on. That's what I heard. And Virginia heard it, too. So when the time is right, I know I can do it and not worry about being true to Jimmy or something."

"So now you're looking to move on?"

"I've been trying to do that for the last few months." Amber narrowed her eyes. "Or do you mean, now am I on the prowl for another guy?" She jumped up. "I should have known you'd think that way."

"Why else tell me?"

"I thought you'd be interested in something that happened to me. I should have known better." She headed for the door that led to the elevators.

"Wait." Adam rose and followed her.

"I don't think so," she said, continuing. Unfortunately, the elevator didn't immediately respond when she pressed the down button. He caught up with her easily.

"I didn't mean you were out trying to snag some guy. I meant, now you can move on without feeling guilty about everything."

"How did you know I feel guilty about everything?" she asked, startled. No one else had picked up on that.

He gave a half smile. "Honey, your emotions show clearly in your face, from happy to sad to guilty. Plus I know something of what you're going through, remember? My mom died. The first time I laughed after her death, I felt like the worst guy in the world. How could I laugh when my mother was dead?"

"Exactly," she said. "Or like kissing someone else when my husband of only a few months was dead."

"Oh." Adam looked flummoxed by that comment.

The elevator arrived, the door sliding slowly open.

She stepped inside. He followed. When the door closed, he pressed the button for her floor.

"Coming to visit?" she asked. She felt daring tonight. Hearing Jimmy's last words, being with Bets all day, had freed her. Maybe she'd explore this friendship and see where it led.

"I wanted to talk to you about moving," he said. "I was at the station today and four other guys have agreed to help. We can go as early as Tuesday, if that works for you."

So much for being daring, Amber thought. He couldn't wait to get rid of her.

"I was having lunch with Virginia on Tuesday, but I'll postpone that. Don't want to waste manpower when it's available."

"Want to go out to dinner?" Adam asked when the elevator reached her floor.

"What? Wouldn't that seem like I was pursuing you?"

"Cut it out, Amber. I didn't mean that. You know my position, I know yours. We both have to eat. Why not together?"

"Dinner out on a Saturday night sounds too much like a date," she said slowly.

They walked to her apartment and she opened the door. Adam followed her in. He looked around, as if judging the number of boxes and how long it would take him and his friends to move them.

"Not a date. You don't date, you're a widow, remember?" he teased.

She threw him a dark look and went to get her purse. It was after six. By the time they got anywhere, it would be time to eat.

"Where to?" she asked.

"What do you like?"

"My favorite is Chinese."

"Then Chinatown it is."

Amber relished soaring up San Francisco's steep hills, and down. The wind blew her hair in the open car. She almost laughed with joy. The baby kicked and rolled, as if enjoying the sensations as well.

Before long they were in the narrow streets of Chinatown. Adam parked in a city lot and took her hand to join the throng that crowded the sidewalk. A favorite tourist attraction, Chinatown was crowded with natives and visitors alike. He led her to a small establishment off

Grant Avenue. Entering, they had to walk up a flight of stairs to reach the restaurant. By the time they were seated, Amber noted they were the only Caucasians in the crowd.

"Must be good," she murmured.

"I think so. What would you like?"

After they ordered, he asked about Corporal Collins' visit. She told him some of the stories Will had shared. "I think I understand a little better why Jimmy liked his job so much, and preferred to spend time on the Army base rather than with me."

Adam shook his head.

"What?"

"Maybe you understand it, but I don't. Why wouldn't he want to spend every minute he could with you?"

She smiled at the compliment. Looking at Adam, Amber realized she didn't know as much about the man as she'd like. Even just friends shared more.

"So tell me about your work, about why you became a firefighter. Did you always want to be a fireman when you were growing up?"

He shook his head. "At one point I wanted to be an astronaut. Another time I thought I'd like to be some gazillionaire. But a neighboring apartment building in Fresno burned when I was fourteen. Two people lost their lives, several families lost all they had in the world. I'll never forget the work the firefighters did to try to save everything—possessions and people alike. The feeling they must have had when they succeeded in saving two-thirds of the building and apartments had to be great. That was when I thought I'd like to do that—help people, make a difference."

"And have you?" She still couldn't understand men and women risking their lives in such a dangerous pursuit.

Granted, saving lives was worthwhile, but to her, all the possessions in the world didn't equal the risk of one person's life.

"A few times. Once I received my E.M.T. certificate, I started going on patrols once every few months to keep current. I've delivered a baby. What a high that was."

She smiled. "Tell me."

Dinner passed swiftly as Adam regaled her with the adventures of his world. She marveled at the things he'd done from delivering the baby, to saving two lives, one a heart-attack victim and another who was choking. She wondered if he glossed over the dangers when he told her about some of the fires they fought. He already knew she thought his job was highly dangerous. Maybe he sugarcoated things to make it seem not so.

Adam knew he was bragging, but he wanted Amber to be impressed. And to understand why he liked his work, felt compelled to do only this job. If she could understand, maybe she wouldn't be so worried about the dangers. He tried to explain how their training was ongoing. How the buddy system had everyone watching out for each other. How the captain would never deliberately put his crew into a situation beyond what they could handle.

And if she saw how much good they did, it had to outweigh the danger.

Dinner was long finished when he slowed down.

"I've probably bored you to tears," he said, noting the time.

"Not at all, and you know it. I'm fascinated. Horrified a time or two, I have to admit. I can't decide whether to admire you to death, or be fearful the next time I hear a siren. Don't you worry the next call will be your last?"

"Amber, most firefighters retire from their jobs, not die in the field."

She shivered. "That may be true, but it doesn't stop all the deaths that happen in spite of all the precautions you talked about."

He didn't want her to focus on that. He wanted her more open about his job.

"Ready to go?" he asked.

She nodded.

He quickly settled the bill, and took her hand as they exited the restaurant. The lights from all the shops on Grant Avenue made the street almost as bright as day.

"Want to walk a bit?"

"Sure."

Adam was pleased she wasn't in a hurry to return home. He wanted her to enjoy the evening, not just have dinner and return to their separate flats.

For the first time ever, he considered asking a woman to move in with him. Without his job to go to, he was lonely. Amber met a need he didn't know he'd had. Different from the camaraderie at the station. A longing rose that was hard to define. Lust? Desire?

Or the yearning for permanency?

CHAPTER EIGHT

TUESDAY morning Bets arrived before eight.

"What are you doing here?" Amber asked, greeting her friend,

"I took a day off to help with the move."

"Oh, no you didn't. You wanted to see Adam," Amber said, laughing. She hugged her friend. "But whatever the reason, I'm glad to see you."

"Here, bagels and lattes," Bets said, holding out a white bag. The hot drinks were balanced on a cardboard tray. "We can eat and then I'll have enough strength to help however you can use me."

"We just might have time to eat. Adam and his friends will be here at nine."

Bets surveyed the stacked boxes, the bed already stripped of its linens.

"You seem ready."

"As ever. By the time my folks get home tomorrow, I'll be only a few blocks from their place, and settled in. I will still need more furniture, and all the baby stuff."

"Does it seem strange going back to where you grew up?"

"Yes, especially since the things I remember won't be there. Mom got rid of a lot of the furniture when she and

Matt bought new things together. But I have my furnishings, and a couple of items I liked from our place. Think how spacious it'll feel without a lot of stuff."

Promptly at nine, Amber heard a knock at the door. She and Bets had eaten, then begun putting the kitchenette items into boxes and bags.

Adam grinned at her when she opened the door and her heart tripped into double time. His eyes seemed to stare right down into her soul. That smile had every fiber of her being focused on him.

"Ready to rock and roll?" he asked.

She glanced behind him where several tall, muscular men filled the hall.

"Come in. I'm as ready as I'll ever be."

The next few moments were taken up with introductions. Amber was bemused by the tiny apartment full of robust, healthy young men. They all resembled Adam in their size and fitness. Bart was tall and dark. Jed was blond, and so tanned Amber knew he had to spend his off time at the beach. He looked like a surfer. Trevor and Brandon were almost interchangeable with their short brown hair and infectious grins. Trevor's wife Jill was also introduced.

"I thought you might need some balance to the testosterone overload," she said with a laugh. "These guys can be intimidating if you don't know them."

Bets was introduced and flattered by some of the compliments she heard from the men. She, Jill and Amber hit it off perfectly and were soon laughing together as if they'd all been friends for years.

Adam took charge, despite some teasing from the other men. In short order, the pile of boxes disappeared.

"You're riding with me," he said to Amber when the last

box left in Bart's strong arms. "You'll have to show us how to get to the apartment and let us in."

"I'm ready," she said.

"We'll keep packing the kitchen stuff," Bets said as she and Jill worked together.

"Then we'll move to the bathroom. The rest is gone, right?" Jill asked.

"Except for the furniture. Wow, I can't believe I'll be all moved before dinner."

"Oh, yeah," Jill said. "That way we get to all go out together and have fun."

Amber smiled and followed Adam. They led the small caravan through the city streets. Bart, Trevor and Brandon all had pickup trucks they'd volunteered. Each was packed high with boxes, tied down for safety.

Of course there was no parking in front of the apartment, one reason Amber had never longed for a car. But there was a loading zone, so two of the pickups swooped into the space. Brandon double-parked. When Adam dropped Amber off, he told her to let Brandon know as soon as he parked, he'd be back to stay with the truck while Brandon helped the others unload. His frustration at limited mobility due to his arm was evident. Amber patted his shoulder and smiled.

"I'm sure you'll have many chances to help out. Let your friends do it today," she said.

He scowled at her. She laughed and headed off to unlock the apartment.

Two more trips and her entire household was moved. The men set up the furniture exactly where she wanted it. Jill and Bets helped her unpack the kitchen and bath. Both were huge in comparison to the ones in her studio apartment. She felt like she'd won the jackpot with the spaciousness of the apartment and so many people helping.

It was only late afternoon when everyone finished, but when Brandon asked if they were ready for dinner, everyone yelled yes.

"Where do we go?" Trevor asked.

Jill rolled her eyes and smiled at Amber. "Wait for it."

"Tony's!" the men yelled.

"Tony's?" Amber asked.

"Home away from home," Bart said.

"Pizza," Adam explained. "A place near the station. Best pizza in the city."

"I'll treat," Amber said. She was quickly outvoted when the men said no way would they let her pay. They were glad for the exercise. And for a chance to meet Adam's new girl.

She looked at him, hoping the panic that hit didn't show.

He shrugged, amusement evident. Leaning close, he brushed back her hair and whispered in her ear, "Let them think what they want, we know the truth."

"Hey, none of that. Wait until you're alone," Jed said, nudging Adam. "Let's go eat, I'm starving."

The firefighters laughed. Apparently Jed was perpetually hungry.

Tony's was a typical pizza parlor with large tables, a jukebox playing popular tunes, and lots of noise. They commandeered a large round table near the back. Pitchers of soft drinks soon appeared, and orders were placed for several large pizzas with the works. Bets sat between Jed and Bart, Jill between Trevor and Brandon, with Amber beside Brandon and Adam on the other side. Before the pizza arrived, however, Jill switched with Brandon and sat beside Amber.

"It's hard to have a normal conversation when these guys are celebrating," Jill said.

"Celebrating my move." Amber shook her head. "What else do they celebrate?"

"You name it and they find a cause to celebrate." Jill looked at them all for a few moments, then at Amber. "They're tight, you know? Have to be, doing the kind of work they do. I think it's amazing how fast Adam fit in. He's only been at this station since May. The others have been here for years."

"Scary job," Amber murmured, studying the men. They were confident, bordering on arrogant. Maybe they had the right. They faced death daily, and won. She shivered.

"Maybe, but they're trained for it. And better they do what they love than be stuck in some job they'd hate. Life wouldn't hold much meaning then, would it?" Jill said.

"Don't you worry about Trevor?"

"Every day. But he wouldn't be who he was if he didn't do what he loved," she said. "I wouldn't want to change him. I love him just as he is."

Amber kept her eyes from Adam. She would not look at him, though the urge to do so was strong. She did not love him. She would not love him. He was merely a neighbor who helped her out. After dinner, she'd go back to her apartment near Van Ness, and he'd return to the one near the University and they'd probably not see each other again.

The thought almost stole her appetite.

Despite working hard all day, no one was in a hurry to end the evening. The tall tales and jokes the men told entertained them all. Bets was in heaven, throwing out jokes and telling funny stories about her own work and efforts to get a college education.

Amber had the best time she'd ever had, sitting back and enjoying the fun that swirled around. She and Jill made plans to get together for lunch before the group finally broke up at almost midnight.

"I can't believe it's so late," she said when the others had said goodbye and left her and Adam on the sidewalk in front of the restaurant. He was driving her home.

"Time flies when you're having fun," Adam said, slinging his good arm around her shoulders as they walked to his car.

Amber leaned against him a little, feeling safe and secure. She was tired, but in a pleasant way.

"Thank you again for all your help."

"If you say that one more time tonight, I swear I'll do something drastic," he said.

"Like what?"

"Like this." He stopped, turned to face her and took her into his arms, kissing her long and deep.

"Oh," she said endless moments later when he raised his head.

"You've thanked us enough times. It was our pleasure to help you out."

"The others didn't even know me."

"They still like helping out. And now they know you. So if you need help in the future, don't hesitate to call."

Amber doubted she'd need their services for anything ever again. But it felt nice to have Adam say they'd come if she called.

The entire evening had been special—because of Adam. He'd made sure she was included. Laughed when she'd told a funny story, and just been beside her the entire time. Occasionally he'd touched her, brushing against her arm when reaching for more drinks, or linking fingers with hers on the bench after they'd finished eating.

Amber was afraid she was falling for the man, and she couldn't let that happen. Ever. She couldn't go through losing a special person in her life again. Not any time soon at least. Maybe when she was eighty.

When they reached the apartment, she was reluctant to go inside. But there was no handy parking place, and who knew how far away they'd find one.

"I'll say good-night here and run on up," she said when he pulled into the loading zone.

"I can park here long enough to see you to your door." He climbed out and went to her door, opening it and reaching for her hand.

Amber didn't want him to go, but it was late. Despite his cast, he'd done a lot in the move. She knew he had to be tired. She was.

"Good night, Amber," he said at the door, kissing her again.

Wednesday Amber finished putting things to suit herself. It was her apartment now, not her mother's. Though by the end of the day, it resembled the home she'd known as a child. Which wasn't all bad; at least she knew where everything was.

She called Virginia to let her know she had moved in, arranging to have lunch on Friday after her appointment with the doctor. She left a message at her mother's to let her know she'd moved.

Then, at loose ends, Amber went for a walk, to refamiliarize herself with the neighborhood.

It was a short walk to Fort Mason and the Bay. She sat

on steps overlooking the water and remembered the roof garden in her old apartment house. Would Adam be up there now, staring out to the ocean?

Maybe she should call him to thank him again for his help yesterday. She laughed. "Right, like he didn't make it clear last night I'd said thank you enough." Thinking about his kiss had her yearning for more.

Sighing, she rose and began to walk. Exercise was good for her and the baby. She wanted to be the best mother in the world. Or second best, after her own.

The next afternoon her mother called to let her know they were home, and to invite her to dinner to tell her about their fabulous trip to Greece.

Amber gladly accepted. She was frankly bored and wanted some company.

Her mother looked radiant when she greeted Amber that evening.

"The baby's bedroom looks wonderful. How did you ever get it all set up yourself?"

"I had help," Amber said, returning her hug.

"Oh?" Sara asked, looking at Matt. "Did someone from Matt's work come over? Dex, maybe?"

"No, it was Adam Carruthers. My neighbor." Amber went to sit down.

"Oh, that was nice." Sara seemed at a loss.

"We appreciate both of you taking care of that. The room is all ready now for the baby," Matt said, filling the awkward silence.

"So tell me all about your trip," Amber said, hoping to change the subject.

"You have got to go to Greece. It's the most wonderful

place on the earth," said Sara, her whole face alight with enthusiasm. "The beaches are incredible, the people so warm and friendly, and the food is delicious. The hotel was exotic. Our room was fantastic."

Amber laughed.

"So you liked it, huh?"

"I did. So did Matt, right?" Sara asked, slanting her husband a sexy look.

"Yes, but I suggest you not give her a play by play recap of everything we did."

Sara blushed and shook her head. "Just the touristy things," she teased.

Amber smiled, enjoying the interaction between her parents.

Her parents. Matt was now her stepfather. She wasn't sure how to react to him sometimes. He was only fourteen years older than she was, but a world of experience separated them. He was perfect for her mother—who had never looked so happy. Once again Amber was struck by envy. She wished she had a special someone who would look at her as if she was the greatest thing on the face of the earth.

"Sara told me you've already moved. How did you manage that?" Matt asked.

"Adam rounded up some of his friends from the fire station and between us all, we moved in no time."

"Adam, again," Sara said.

"He's just a neighbor, Mom."

"Not anymore."

Amber nodded.

When they sat down for dinner, after hearing about Sara and Matt's trip to Greece, Amber told them about her visit from Corporal Collins. And about Virginia driving her crazy.

"She needs a hobby," Amber grumbled.

"So suggest one," Sara said. "You know some of her friends, don't you? Ask them to invite her to lunch or something. Sometimes it's hard to get back into the swing of things after being out of touch for a while."

"Maybe, but I still wish I could find something for her to do that would focus some of her attention away from me," Amber said.

They arranged to meet the next morning at the doctor's office. Amber said she had errands to run so would meet them there, rather than have Matt pick her up as he'd offered.

"Going to let them tell you the sex of the baby?" Sara asked as Amber was leaving.

"Yes. I think I will."

"Me, too. Tomorrow we'll know!"

There was a message from Virginia on her answering machine when she returned to her apartment. Amber had hoped maybe Adam would have called to see how she was doing. But he hadn't. She couldn't think up a good reason to call him. They had exchanged phone numbers on Tuesday. Maybe she should have withheld that as a reason to call.

Once she found out what gender her baby would be, she'd call him and tell him. He'd want to know, wouldn't he? On impulse, Amber invited Virginia to join her at the doctor's the next morning. They could go to lunch together after the visit, since their Tuesday lunch had been canceled.

"I was sure it would be a boy," Virginia said when they sat down to lunch at the Tea Garden Restaurant on Van Ness shortly after one o'clock the next afternoon.

"Are you disappointed?" Amber asked, thrilled to know

her daughter would be born before Thanksgiving, if the doctor was right.

"I guess not." Virginia tried to put on a brighter face. "I just never thought about a girl. I thought it'd be a boy, like Jimmy."

"But this isn't Jimmy." Amber wondered if Virginia had thought the baby would be just like her son—a replacement almost. "It's part of Jimmy, but part of me and my family as well. It might be better to have a girl, we won't be looking for her to be so much like he was."

Virginia nodded. "Sometimes, Amber, you are wise beyond your years. I think I'll just have a light meal today. I want to get home to James."

"Call him, tell him the news if you like. Lunch can wait."

"No, I'll tell him when I get home."

"So do you want to come to the hospital with me when I go for the tour?" Amber asked, trying to make up for the other woman's obvious disappointment. Amber was delighted with whatever the baby would be, and it had been a lovely surprise when the doctor told her this morning the baby was female. She mainly wanted a healthy baby.

But for a split second, she'd wished for a rowdy little boy, getting in and out of trouble. Would she find someone one day to marry and have a family with? Would she get her little boy with dark eyes and dark hair?

Adam immediately came to mind. She pushed the image away. She hadn't seen nor heard from him since Tuesday night. Now that they were no longer neighbors, she didn't expect to hear from him often.

Who was she kidding? She wanted to hear from him every day. Suddenly she looked at Virginia and realized she wanted what this woman had, a loving husband and devoted father. She wanted the closeness her mother and Matt shared. She wanted someone to love and to be loved by.

And she wished with all her heart it was Adam Carruthers.

"No," she said involuntarily.

"What?" Virginia looked up from the menu.

"I mean, no fattening stuff for me. I'll join you and have a salad as well."

"I thought you'd take the hospital tour with your mother," Virginia said after they'd placed their orders.

"She'll be going with Matt. I'd like someone to go with me," Amber said.

"I'd be delighted. Thank you for asking me," Virginia said rather formally.

"I'll call you as soon as I make the appointment. What day works best for you?"

They discussed the tour, the news about the baby being a girl, and argued slightly over the furnishings yet again.

"Tell you what, why don't you work with Kathy and Bets on the baby shower? They're throwing one for me in late September at Kathy's place. You remember Kathy, don't you? She went to school with Jimmy and me."

"The red-haired girl with a million freckles?" Virginia guessed.

"Right. She's pregnant, too. Her baby is due any day. She said she'd be ready to give the shower easily by the time the date arrives, but I'm sure there are things that need to be done beforehand."

"I'd love to," Virginia said.

Amber breathed a sigh of relief. Maybe she could find other things for Virginia to do that would help her occupy her and leave less time for dwelling on Amber and the coming grandchild.

When Amber returned home it was late afternoon. She called Adam, anxious to speak with him. His answering machine picked up. Slowly Amber hung up. She wanted to talk to him, not leave some message. She'd try later.

Amber tried three more times before going to bed that night. She didn't leave any messages. She'd rather catch him than wait or look needy by calling after she left the message.

Saturday morning Amber was busy vacuuming the empty bedroom in preparation for getting the furniture. She had bought some curtains she liked, and bedding to go with them. Her plans today included shopping for furniture, and a few things like diapers and bibs. She wanted to wait until after her friends threw her a baby shower to see what she got there that she wouldn't need to buy herself. Money wasn't that lavish that she could duplicate things.

When she heard the knock on the door, she thought her mother had dropped by. She hoped it was that, and not Virginia.

Adam stood in the doorway when she opened the door.

"Hi," he said, stepping inside. "Busy?"

"Hi yourself," Amber said, shutting the door and looking at him. She could study him all day. He looked fit and even darker tanned than the last time she'd seen him. His cast was still in evidence, but otherwise he looked as fit as ever.

"What are you doing here?" she asked.

"Came to see if you wanted to do something today."

"I was thinking of going shopping for baby things," she said, ready to cancel at a moment's notice if Adam wanted to do something. Being with him would be more fun.

"I guess you need to get things going with that," he said.

"I guess. It's not like I can change my mind or anything. Besides, I can't wait to see my daughter."

"It's a girl?" he asked.

"I found out yesterday," she said.

"You should have called me," he said.

Amber cleared her throat nervously. "Actually I did."

"I wasn't home. You could have left a message."

"I guess. Where were you?"

"Went to the station. They're shorthanded on the ambulance crew, so I helped out with paperwork. Never the fun part of the job, but it got me out of the house."

"Getting cabin fever?" she teased.

"You know it. Can't wait to get back to work." He held up his arm. "It's healing good, the doctor said. I saw him on Thursday. Might get a limited release in the next week or two—for light work, not normal activities. But heck, something is better than nothing."

"I wouldn't be so impatient to get back into your line of work."

He ruffled her hair. "You worry too much. I'll be fine."

"Maybe, or maybe not. Isn't there something else you could do that wouldn't be so dangerous?"

"Like what? Be a dispatcher?" His demeanor changed. The amusement that usually lurked in his eyes was missing. He didn't like talking about changing jobs, she could tell that instantly.

"Not a dispatcher. What about—" Amber's mind went blank. She couldn't picture Adam in a suit and tie in some dull job in the city. Maybe a construction worker. Until she pictured him climbing up the high-rise buildings that were going up around the city. That didn't seem any safer.

"Never mind. Want to come shopping with me?"

"What do I know about baby furniture?"

"Probably as much as I do. But you might have pointers from things you've seen on the job that I wouldn't think of."

He seemed to weigh the pros and cons of her invitation then slowly smiled. Amber felt her insides turn over.

"I'll come shopping if we finish by noon. Then we can take a ride up the coast, and be back in time for dinner at Trevor's. Jill wanted me to bring you over."

It was just after nine o'clock in the morning. Adam wanted to spend the entire day with her—including dinner?

"Let me change quickly and I'll be ready," she said.

Adam thought she looked fine just the way she was, but he realized women had different outlooks on things. He wandered around the living room. She'd hung pictures on the walls, better seen in this room than in the studio she'd had before. Or maybe the pictures hadn't been in the old apartment. He didn't remember them.

He looked into the kitchen. It was larger than his. Perhaps he could get her to offer to cook a couple of meals for him. It didn't take as long as he'd thought it would to get from his apartment to hers. Not as convenient as running down a flight of stairs, however.

He went to the window and looked out over the busy street. He'd missed her. Clenching a fist, he raised his arm and rested it against the window edge, staring out, seeing nothing. He hadn't expected to miss her so much when she moved. It had been all he could do to keep from calling her every day this week. She'd only been gone four days. He couldn't believe the hole she'd left.

It wasn't as if they were dating or anything. Or had even known each other for that long, come to that.

But there was something about Amber that had gotten beneath his skin, and he wasn't sure that was going away.

She was meant for love and family and babies. A home full of laughter and commotion and activities that revolved around family.

He'd been alone a long time, even before his mother died.

"Ready," she said.

He turned slowly and looked at her. She was beautiful. Obviously pregnant, but not huge yet, she had the glow that he'd heard pregnant women got. Her smile was infectious, and he felt the kick of attraction deep inside. He wanted her. He wished he could see that blond hair spread on his pillow with her eyes shining up at him. He'd love to touch and taste that satiny skin, run his fingers through her silky hair, and lock the world outside, making a place for only the two of them.

He shook his head slowly. He was losing his mind.

"Something wrong?" Amber asked.

"Not a thing. Baby store here we come."

Adam couldn't believe he'd said that. He knew nothing about babies, or children in general. He'd never expected to have any, since usually a wife was first required. He could change that, by staying in touch with Amber. She'd invite him over to see her new daughter, and he would go, to see the mother.

He felt like he was playing with fire—exposing himself to the flames, dancing away when he felt himself drawn too close. Would he get singed? Or worse, hurt her in some way?

CHAPTER NINE

ADAM felt like a bull in a china shop in the baby store. It was huge, with everything imaginable for babies, from car seats to cribs to toys and clothing.

"Big business," he murmured following Amber to the furniture section.

"People always have families," she said. "First-time parents especially want everything for their new baby. I was going to get some secondhand things, but Matt insisted on paying for new."

He looked at some of the tiny clothes hanging from racks as they passed by. Did babies really come that small? They looked as if they'd fit dolls.

Amber seemed to know exactly what she wanted for her baby, and was soon discussing pros and cons with the salesclerk, glancing at Adam once in a while. "What do you think?" she asked.

"Whatever you want," he said.

The clerk beamed. Undoubtedly the man thought Adam was a doting husband and father-to-be. He had an urge to set him straight, but hesitated. It didn't matter. He'd never see the guy again after today. Why make things awkward?

"Is that everything?" the salesclerk said, checking his list.

"I want a glider rocker like my mother got here recently," Amber said, walking over to a row of rockers. She sat in one and moved back and forth, then rose and tried another.

Adam watched her. For a moment when she pretended she was holding a baby to test the armrests, he pictured her with a child of his. Dark hair and eyes, lusty cry, fretful until his mother soothed him and fed him.

He looked away and scowled. He was not going down that road. What if the worst did happen and he was killed at his job? Did he want some woman to be left alone with kids, struggling to make it, like his mother had been? Like Amber was since Jimmy died?

Only, Amber wasn't struggling. She had herself together, had set goals, and had a loving support network surrounding her. She was stronger at this young age than his mother had ever been.

The salesclerk finished writing up the order and discussing delivery dates with Amber.

"Make it next Tuesday and I'll be there to set it up," he said, stepping into the conversation. He didn't like the way the man was looking at Amber. Couldn't he see she was pregnant? Didn't seem to matter, he was definitely interested in her. Time Adam let him know she was not available.

"Of course, sir," the clerk said, stepping back hastily. He looked at Adam and immediately stepped back another foot. "I just need an address and contact phone, in case the delivery runs late."

Amber took Adam's arm as the clerk left to confirm the order. "What's the matter with you? You looked as if you wanted to chew him up and spit him out."

"He was flirting with you."

"He was not."

"Yes, he was."

Amber frowned. "He was? He couldn't be, I'm pregnant."

"So? You're still a beautiful woman."

"You're nuts. Wait another month or two and say that."

"I probably will," he muttered.

They took his car and drove north on Highway One, heading for the redwoods. Amber loved driving with the top down. She had lots to think about as Adam competently handled the convertible through the twists and turns in the road. He'd called her beautiful. And actually thought a stranger would flirt with her. How cool was that? Not that she wanted anyone to flirt with her. But the mere thought she wasn't invisible any longer intrigued her.

Did Adam want to flirt with her?

She looked at him. Did she want to flirt with him?

Jimmy had been gone longer than the few months since his death. She was young, healthy and falling for the man next to her. Could she make him change his mind about his job?

She turned to watch the trees whiz by. No, she couldn't move Adam from his chosen path. That wouldn't make a good relationship. If he did that, in time he'd come to resent her. And she wasn't sure she wanted a long-term relationship with a man who would give in to her every whim. Not that she didn't like getting her own way in things, but she didn't need it all the time.

Could she bear to have him leave each day and be scared all the time he wouldn't come home? She had had that basic trust shattered by Jimmy's death. It wasn't something she'd regain soon.

When they arrived at Muir Woods, Amber looked at him.

"We're going hiking?"

"After we eat. They have a nice deli here that serves terrific sandwiches. Then I thought we could take one of the walks. They're easy—even for a pregnant woman."

"I love it here," Amber said. "I've only been a couple of times, but it seems a world away from San Francisco."

"It's one of my favorite places," Adam said, getting out of the car.

Muir Woods was an old-growth forest of Coast Redwoods. The climate was a microcosm away from San Francisco's, and usually cooler than the surrounding countryside.

The tall redwoods towered above them, shading everything, allowing dappled sunlight to spot the forest floor.

Lunch was quick and before long Amber walked along the level wide path of beaten dirt, lined on both sides by split rail fencing. Adam reached for her hand.

"You're not too cold are you?" he asked. "It's cooler here than in the city."

"I'm fine." With his hand wrapped around hers, she was toasty warm. And her heart was beating fast enough to keep her blood warm all day. She tried to enjoy the walk. Her awareness of Adam escalated. As if the mere thought of a kiss conjured up the notion in his head, he stopped on a deserted spot of the trail and leaned over to kiss her.

Amber wished the quick brush of lips had evolved into more, but they were in a public venue and other visitors to the park could come by at any moment.

She had never come with Jimmy, only with her mother. Adam's bringing her was special. And she vowed to enjoy every moment of the experience.

By the time they drove back to the city heading for Trevor and Jill's, Amber was growing tired. She'd already had a full day, and the further along she got in her pregnancy, the more quickly she became fatigued. Yet she never suggested that Adam call and cancel. She looked forward to seeing Jill again, and seeing the interaction between Adam and his friends.

It gave her greater insight into the man himself, though she was playing with fire learning more about him. So far it had all been to the good. He would make a wonderful partner, and, she suspected, a wonderful father. But she needed to keep things in perspective. He was not interested in a relationship, and certainly not marriage. She wasn't either, so friends it was.

Trevor and Jill greeted her warmly. Jill invited her into the kitchen while she finished preparing the meal, while the men stayed in the living room.

"So, are you all settled in the new apartment?" Jill asked.

"Pretty much," Amber said, sitting on the high stool indicated at the breakfast bar, watching Jill whip around her kitchen. "Can I help?"

"Nope, but I do like the company."

"We went shopping for baby furniture today," Amber said.

"We?"

"Adam and I."

Jill smiled. "Good. I was hoping you two were hitting it off. He's a great guy and needs someone special."

Amber was startled at the comment.

"We're just friends."

"Best kind of marriages are between friends who are also lovers, don't you think?" Jill asked.

"Marriage? There's no talk of that between us. I hardly know the man. And there are complications."

Jill looked up. "Oh, I'm so sorry. I almost forgot about your husband. Of course it's too soon, and all. I'm not saying you two will rush off to Tahoe and get married right away."

Amber thought about the last time she ran off to Tahoe to get married. She and Jimmy had rushed through a wedding, but never really built a marriage. If she ever took the plunge again, it would definitely not include a Lake Tahoe wedding.

"Adam doesn't want to get married."

Jill shrugged.

"And I don't want to marry a firefighter," Amber said firmly.

The other woman looked up at that.

"Why ever not? They're terrific. And really hot lovers." She laughed at her joke.

"Don't you worry every day when Trevor leaves that he may not come back?" Amber asked.

Jill shook her head. "Not really. I trust things will be fine. But if not, what am I supposed to do, live in fear for a future that might never come? I want to enjoy life to the fullest right now. I have a great husband, a good job, and if fate is kind, I'll have it all until I'm an old, old woman."

"But what if you don't?"

"Then I don't. But should I miss the love of my life out of worry about what might never happen?" Jill countered.

Love of her life. Amber had at one time thought Jimmy the love of her life. But that had been back when they were in school. Lately, however, she was changing her mind about things. She wondered, if Jimmy had returned, if they would have rediscovered that special spark that had once blazed between them.

"It's hard to lose someone you love," Amber said slowly.

"I bet it is. I haven't had that experience yet," Jill said.

"My grandparents and parents and all are still around. But a person can't just shut down after someone dies, either. It's a normal part of life. Here, help me carry the food in and we'll call the men."

Amber carried the platter of roast beef, went back for vegetables. Jill carried in the potatoes and rolls. When she called Trevor and Adam, they quickly joined them.

Amber thought there was enough food to feed a small army, but with the two men it quickly disappeared.

Jill and Trevor kept her entertained. Trevor loved to tell stories about the fire station. Adam didn't play a part in most of them, he'd transferred recently to this station so was still considered the new kid on the block. He'd act defensive sometimes, but by the twinkle in his eye, Amber knew he was just playing along with Trevor.

It was late by the time Adam suggested they leave. Amber had been tired earlier, but had found her second wind, and thoroughly enjoyed the evening.

"They are so fun to be with," she said when Adam pulled away from the curb, driving toward her place.

"I know. Trevor is funny at work, too. Keeps things from getting too serious at times."

"Are all the men like that? You seem to keep a bright outlook on life."

"It's a great life, why wouldn't I? There are as many different personalities as there are men and women working at the station. Most are optimistic, I think. Aren't you?"

Amber felt her usual outlook was definitely more positive than negative. Though she'd lost some of that over the last months. "I think so. Even when I get knocked down, I come back." She was surprised to realize she had come back. She still mourned Jimmy's passing, and as her mother said, would probably always miss him. But she was looking to the future, to the birth of her daughter, and getting her teaching credential.

"Thank you for a wonderful time," she said when Adam pulled into the loading zone before her apartment.

"I'll be back on Tuesday to set up the furniture," he said.

"You don't have to," she said.

"Yes, I do." He brushed back her hair, threading his fingers into the softness and pulled her closer. His kiss was gentle, sweet and far too short.

Tuesday morning Adam woke with a feeling of anticipation. He hadn't seen Amber in three days. And as far as he was concerned, that was three days too long. He wished she hadn't moved across town. It was one thing to run into her in the same apartment, or even at the park, something else again to run into her across town. She'd know he'd come just to see her.

"Is that so wrong?" he asked as he shaved. Being with her made him happier.

He stared at his reflection. Was that what love was about? Not making someone else happy, but finding happiness in their company? Was he falling in love with a widow who never wanted to marry again?

He swished the razor in the water and applied himself to shaving. Philosophy so early in the morning wasn't his thing. Yet the more he thought about it, the more he wondered if he could convince her to take a chance—at least let them explore their friendship to see where it would lead.

He had never planned to marry, himself, but if Amber changed his mind, maybe he could change hers.

He banged the cast against the doorjamb in his hurry to get dressed. It didn't even hurt. He flexed his fingers, tightened them into as much of a fist as he could with the plaster covering his palm. A mild ache was all. He was definitely healing.

It wouldn't come fast enough. He was bored with his own company and lack of activity. He would never take perfect health for granted again.

Grabbing a bite to eat, he quickly headed for Amber's place. He couldn't wait to see her again.

When she opened the door a half hour later, Adam felt the punch of seeing her clear through. Her eyes widened when they saw him. He would swear he'd seen a glimmer of happiness. She swept her arm to the side inviting him into the apartment.

"What are you doing here so early?" she asked.

She was dressed. The shorts revealed long slender legs. Her loose top couldn't completely camouflage the growing mound of her stomach. Except for that distinctive bulge, she was still slender.

Her hair was shining, hanging down to her shoulders. He wanted to wrap it around his hands, let the strands flow through his fingers. If he leaned closer, he'd smell that special scent that was Amber's alone. He leaned forward a bit, and she came to meet him, raising her face to his, letting her eyes drift close.

Adam kissed her, stepping in closer, drawing her into his arms. She was so sweet and warm. He wanted to lose himself in her embrace and spend the next millennium without moving.

A short jab to his abdomen had him jerk back.

"What was that?"

Amber giggled, taking his hand and putting it on her stomach.

"Little missy is up and about," she said, holding it on one part. In only seconds, Adam felt the definite movement, and another jab. Awe filled him. This was her baby, moving in the womb, making her presence known. He'd never felt an unborn child before. His eyes locked with hers as they shared the moment. He could feel a poke again, and this time he tried to figure out the shape—a foot maybe.

"Does it hurt?"

"No. Sometimes it's a little uncomfortable, and I expect as she grows and the space becomes tighter, it'll be even more, but it doesn't hurt. I think it's cool."

"I do, too."

A few minutes later all activity ceased.

"Over for now, I think," Amber said.

Slowly Adam raised his hands to cup her face. He kissed her, in longing and in gratitude for sharing.

He was breathing hard when he pulled back. This wasn't the time or the place to follow through. She was still hurting from her husband's death, and the deliverymen could show up at any moment.

"Want some coffee?" she asked.

Adam was pleased to note she was breathing as hard as he was. Her mouth was rosy from his kiss, and her eyes still held the mysterious look women got when they were caught in the moment.

He didn't want coffee, he wanted her. Or a cold shower.

"Fine," he said, walking across the living room to the small hallway and into the baby's room. The curtains were on the windows. Otherwise it was empty. Soon to be filled with the furniture they'd selected last weekend.

He wanted to do more than set up the furniture. He wanted to make a contribution for the baby. But her parents had bought about all she needed. At least he could put it together.

"I can't believe soon I'll have a little girl sleeping in here," she said from the doorway, holding out a mug of hot coffee.

He took it and nodded, thinking she looked too young to be a mother.

"You going to be able to manage school in the fall?"

"I think so. I might have to take delayed finals, but I'm hoping I can keep up. If not, then I'll just take the course work over in the spring. It'll set back my graduation, but I can handle that."

"Who will watch the baby?"

She turned and led the way back into the living room. "That's still open for discussion. Virginia wanted to raise the baby altogether. Or at least she did before she found out it was a girl."

"What does that mean?"

"I think she thought it'd be a little boy just like Jimmy. That she could relive his childhood through his son."

"It wouldn't be the same."

"I know that. I think she does, too, now. So she's a possible."

"And your mother?"

"Until they start traveling. She's really got a case of wanderlust. Whatever happens, I'm sure I'll find someone."

For one startling moment, Adam thought he'd volunteer. He'd love to watch Amber's child. He could take her to the fire station and show her off. Take her to the beach and watch as the baby stared at the ocean with wide eyes, or followed a seagull as it soared above them.

He looked away. He was losing it. Too much inactivity had atrophied his brain. He wasn't a baby person. He was a firefighter. A lone wolf who liked the status quo just fine.

He sat on the sofa and sipped the hot coffee. The sooner the furniture arrived, the sooner he'd have something to do besides give way to flights of fantasy.

Amber brought out some cinnamon rolls and sat in the chair near the sofa.

It was midmorning when the furniture was delivered. Because Amber had chosen a simpler style than her mother, the bed and rocker were quickly assembled. Adam tightened every bolt securely, made sure the sides moved smoothly, and tested the rocker. If it would hold him, it would hold Amber.

"How is it?" she asked as he was rocking. She brought sheets from her room and was making up the bed.

"Works fine."

"I know I'll have to wash these again by the time she's born, but I think it makes the room look finished," she said, smoothing the cotton over the small mattress.

Adam watched her as she worked, his temporary respite from wanting over. When she leaned over, he wanted to cup her bottom and feel the firm curves. When she straightened, and arched back a bit, his palms itched to hold her breasts in them, to caress the skin he knew had to be as soft as down.

He stood abruptly, this was driving him crazy. Either get on with it, or walk away.

"Are you hungry?" Amber asked. "I could fix us lunch."

He gathered up the cardboard, bending the larger pieces. "I'm hungry, but let's go out and get something. Save you the work."

"I don't mind."

"Still, let's go." Outside where there were other people, where he could concentrate on other things besides Amber and how delectable she looked.

"Okay, let me wash up."

"I'll take this to your trash area if you tell me where, then come back and wash—" Adam began. The knock on the door interrupted him.

He finished gathering up the trash when she went to open the door. When he heard Virginia Woodworth's voice, he wasn't surprised. Amber had the patience of a saint to put up with the woman.

How would she react to seeing him here? No time like the present to find out.

He lifted all the large pieces, scooping up a couple of the smaller ones as well. Balanced perfectly, he headed out.

"So I said to James..." Virginia's voice trailed off when she spotted Adam.

He almost smiled. He could have orchestrated her reaction.

"What is he doing here?" she asked.

"Adam, you remember Virginia Woodworth, don't you?" Amber said calmly. "Virginia, Adam was helping me put together the baby furniture. Do come and see what I've picked out. I still need more things, but I'll wait a while longer."

Virginia glared at him before following Amber.

Someone could have gotten the door before they left, he thought, trying to find the knob beneath all the folded cardboard. If he didn't keep a grip on it, the pile would fall every which way.

Five minutes later he headed back to the apartment. He'd left the door unlatched, so he could let himself in. He could hear the voices from the baby's room. Bypassing the opportunity to visit more with Virginia, he went to the bathroom to wash his hands.

Girly things were everywhere. He smiled at the pink razor, the bottles of lotions and creams. Did Amber really use everything in sight? Or were all the primping things there for special occasions?

He'd like to see her all dressed up. Maybe he could take her out to celebrate the new furniture. They could go to dinner, then dancing. Maybe head back to his place for a nightcap—and he'd bring her home first thing in the morning.

He splashed cold water on his face, hoping to knock some sense into his head. Amber wasn't the kind of girl who would sleep casually with whoever asked. She was going to be a mother, for heaven's sake. Even if she wasn't, she was the type to expect commitment and a ring.

She had seemed happy to see him this morning, but was that just her polite facade? How could anyone be expected to keep another person happy for a lifetime? Whoever thought up marriage hadn't thought it all through. Too many pitfalls.

But for one instant, Adam almost wished he dare try.

Amber took a breath and tried to hold on to her temper. If Virginia said another word about Adam's being here, she would scream.

"He is a friend who came to assemble the baby's furniture," Amber explained again.

The edge in her voice must have penetrated. Virginia looked at her sharply.

"So you said. James could have done this. Or your new stepfather."

"Matt is busy. I know James could have helped, but Adam volunteered. Firefighters spend their off-hours helping people. He has experience in this kind of thing." If nothing else, he'd practiced on her mother's new furniture.

"It just doesn't look right. People will talk."

Amber almost laughed. "What people?" she asked. It wasn't as if she were some big public figure that everyone clamored to learn more about. As to the people who counted, so far no one seemed to find anything out of the usual. Except Virginia.

"Jimmy's not even been dead for a year."

"I know how long he's been dead. And how long he's been gone. Two different things."

"What do you mean?"

Amber really didn't want to have this talk with Virginia. But maybe she could make her understand a little better if she cleared things up. "Virginia, he left town almost two years ago. Except for a week's leave a year ago, and when we got married in February, I hadn't seen him in all that time. I feel he left then, not when he died."

Virginia looked shocked. "He was just away, not dead."

"I know. But in a way, things all changed when he left. I started college, he embraced his military career. We didn't have the same things in common anymore."

"And you and this Adam have things in common, I suppose," Virginia said.

"Not so much. We are not involved, no matter what you think."

"Not that I wouldn't like us to be," Adam said from the doorway.

CHAPTER TEN

AMBER turned abruptly. "What did you say?"

"When the time's right, maybe we will become more involved." He looked at Virginia as if in challenge. "You don't expect Amber to mourn her husband the rest of her life, do you? She's only twenty. She has a lifetime ahead of her."

"She has a baby to think about now," Virginia said, outraged.

"And the baby will need a father," Adam said gently.

Virginia looked at Amber in horror. "Is that your plan, rush right out and find some other man to be father to Jimmy's child?"

"I don't have any plans right now except to have a healthy baby. As to getting married again, I don't know about that. I'm still grieving for my husband. I don't know if I'll ever risk falling in love again. What if something happens to that man? I don't think I can stand losing someone dear to me again." She looked at them both. "You've each lost someone, but not at my age. Not at my stage in life. It hurts. My entire world has been rocked."

"We all die in the end," Adam said.

"Most of us die when we're old, not before we've had

a chance to live," she retorted. "Anyway, you're a great one to talk. Look at what you do for a living—daring death every day. I don't want to discuss this. Thank you for your help. Goodbye."

Adam didn't move.

"Virginia, I asked you not to badger me so much. We're scheduled for the hospital tour next week, I'll see you then." Amber spun around and pushed past Adam to go to her room. She shut the door and leaned against it. Wasn't Jimmy's death enough to deal with without all the stress of his mother pushing into her life? And what had Adam been thinking when he made that comment—that he wanted to become more involved? Was he deliberately provoking Virginia? Or had he meant it?

She felt almost giddy with the thought. Just how much more involved did he want to be? Not that there'd be any long-term future together. They both had issues that precluded that.

Adam had stood up for her, though. That was something she hadn't expected. Could she get him to change his job to something safer?

Unlikely. He loved his work. She couldn't imagine anyone trying to talk her out of teaching. What if someone suggested she become an accountant or something? She'd hate that.

Pushing away from the door, she went to lie down on her bed, her thoughts jumbled.

"He's right," she said softly, rubbing her stomach. "One day I might consider getting married again."

And if so, she'd like the man to be just like Adam—only with a safe job.

"Except—it's scary falling in love."

There would be the excitement of being with a man she loved. The commitment to share lives and futures. She'd have to make sure. She knew in her mind she didn't want a man with a dangerous profession. Yet her heart yearned for Adam.

"No!" she said aloud. It was too soon to be thinking about marriage again. Yet she couldn't help think how awestruck Adam had been when he felt the baby move. How kind he'd been to help her set up the nursery. How interested he always was when she spoke of her plans, or what she wanted to do for the baby.

He had other friends. But he chose to spend a lot of his time with her. And she relished every moment they had together.

Maybe, just maybe, she was falling for him. She liked spending time with him. Looked forward to the hours they shared. He made her laugh, and made her angry sometimes. But overall, there was a blossom of happiness surrounding her as fragile as gossamer.

Panic clicked in. She couldn't love Adam. She couldn't love anyone. She needed stability, safety. She wanted the quiet ache in her heart to fade completely, not to miss Jimmy so much. To get to the stage where she only remembered the fun they'd had.

She was also making memories with Adam. Would she remember him fondly as the years went by? What if his life was cut tragically short? How could she deal with that?

She missed him already. A phone call would have him back in no time. The better plan, however, was to curtail her time with him. Once his arm was healed and he was back at work, he'd be too busy to spend much time with her.

The apartment was quiet. Sighing, Amber rose. She was hungry. Food would give her the energy to face facts. She wished they'd gone out to lunch as planned. But after her curt goodbye, she'd be lucky if Adam spoke to her again.

She stopped at the edge of the living room in surprise. Adam sat on the sofa, leafing through a magazine. If the surprise hadn't been so great, she might have laughed to see such a macho male studying a woman's magazine with every appearance of fascinated interest.

"I thought you left," she said.

He lifted his head. "I'm not Virginia. She left. We were going to lunch, remember?"

She nodded. "I still thought you left. What if I took your attention for more than you mean? What if I wanted to pursue you, as you are so afraid of?"

He laughed, rose and came toward her. "Pursue away." He pulled her into his arms and kissed her.

Time seemed suspended. The room spun around, and Amber caught hold of the only solid anchor, Adam. Her arms tightened as she pressed herself against him, feeling desire rise, sensations sweep through and ecstasy blossom.

His hands pulled her against him, rubbing her back, setting every cell ablaze. She put her fingers in his hair, feeling the warmth, the thick texture, reveling in the intimacy between them.

When he moved his mouth to trail kisses across her cheek, to her jaw, to that pulse point at the base of her throat, Amber gave herself up to the delights only Adam brought. His muscles were strong; she could feel them moving as his arms moved. His chest was solid, and she relished the strength.

Even the baby seemed to enjoy the man's touch. She was as still as could be as if not to interrupt this special embrace.

Endless moments of delight cascaded, one after the

other. Amber savored every second, relishing the feeling of being alive to Adam's touch as the blood that pounded through her veins affirmed life and love.

The knowledge shot through her—she loved Adam Carruthers, as she'd never loved another, not even Jimmy.

Shocked, Amber pulled away, fear crowding in.

"Stop. We can't do this." She was breathing as hard as if she'd run up the stairs from the street. She couldn't be in love with this man. It was too dangerous, too risky.

Adam just looked at her.

"It's too soon. Too much. We can't get involved. I don't want to be involved."

"Honey, we are involved, and your denying it or my denying it doesn't change it."

"But you don't like the situation," she guessed.

He shrugged. "I told you about my mother. I never want to be responsible for another person's happiness."

"You aren't responsible for anyone but yourself," Amber shot back.

"Unless I get hooked up with some woman who expects me to make her happy."

"Won't you expect her to make you happy in return?" Amber asked.

Adam hesitated a moment, gave it some thought. "I make myself happy. Though I find happiness in unexpected places and with unexpected people."

"Maybe your mother was needier than most. Was she so happy with your father?" She didn't really care, but couldn't deal with their own situation. She wanted to think about something else, anything else.

"I don't know. She remembers being happy with him. But they weren't together that long."

"Maybe she remembered happier days. But she had the ability to find her own happiness. She chose not to."

"And I can choose whichever way I want?" he asked.

"You already have."

"What if I say I'm happy around you?"

"What if I say you're happy around Trevor as well."

He almost smiled at that. "Yeah, Trevor can make me laugh. But you bring happiness."

Amber felt a glow at his compliment. But she didn't want that. She wanted them to go back to being mere acquaintances, without kisses and shared experiences or any attraction. Without these feelings that were filling every inch of her.

"Just being with you, doing mundane things, and I'm happy," he said.

"You look surprised," she commented, feeling that fluttering feeling again. She didn't want this.

"I am. For years I've thought my mother's view of things was the right way. Now I'm not so sure. Ready for lunch?"

Amber was confused at his quick change of subject. But she was relieved to get off the personal and back to the more general. She couldn't be in love with him. It was just infatuation, or hormones. Yes, that was it. Hormones, as Virginia had said a while back. They'd go to lunch, spend another couple of hours together and say goodbye.

Adam did not allude to their relationship over lunch, keeping the conversation safely impersonal. Amber had a harder time turning off her thoughts. Or her feelings.

When he invited her out the following evening, she refused, despite his urging. She was feeling more and more panicked at the feelings that kept surfacing. She needed to back away before she got hurt again. The fun wasn't worth the pain of loss.

She called her mother when she got home.

"Hi, sweetie, what's up?" Sara asked when she recognized her daughter's voice.

"Come see my baby's furniture. Adam set it up today. It looks great."

"I'll be over soon. Is Adam still there?"

"No. We went to lunch, then he took off. Virginia was here earlier."

"I bet that went well if Adam was there."

"She asked me what people would think."

"About?"

"About my seeing someone else so soon after Jimmy's death, of course. Bets thinks I shouldn't act like a nun all my life. Kathy wants to meet him to make sure he's good enough for me. What do you think?"

"Is this Adam important to you?"

Amber closed her eyes, wishing she could say a resounding No! But she was fearful she was in over her head and whichever way she chose would cause heartache—either now or later.

"I don't want him to be," she said at last.

"Why?"

"He's a firefighter. He was hurt in the last fire he worked, he could be killed in the next one. Or the one after that."

"And?"

"I can't go through losing someone I love again. It hurts too much."

Sara was silent for a moment. "We don't always get to choose," she said at last. "And as one who thought my life was set when I was eighteen, and found it completely turned around without any warning, I'd say consider carefully before you make any long-lasting decision. Do remember that not everyone has the chance to fall in love with a wonderful man who will share life's journey with you. Don't throw away something precious."

"I can't do it again, Mom. I can't risk it. You saw me when I learned about Jimmy. I was a wreck. I can't bear that pain again." And she feared it would be worse with Adam. She hadn't known him nearly as long, but her feelings seemed more intense, more mature. She couldn't imagine a world without him in it. How would she ever live through his death?

"Then you have your answer. Do you still want me to come over?"

"Yes. Bring Matt."

"Of course. Where I go, he goes," Sara said. "And hopefully soon where he goes, the baby and I'll go. See you in a few minutes."

Amber hung up. She had her answer. She would call Adam tonight and tell him she didn't wish to see him again.

No, he deserved to have her tell him face-to-face. She wouldn't hide behind a phone that could be quickly hung up. She owed him more than that. It would be the last time she'd see him.

Just the thought was painfully sad. But better sad now than risk devastation later. It wasn't as if he'd been a big part of her life for long. She'd only known him for a few weeks. It wouldn't take long to get over this infatuation.

School would soon be starting. That would take care of the immediate future. Then she had the baby to plan for. If she kept focused on what was important, things would come round. She'd keep her equilibrium and find contentment with her work and her child.

* * *

Afraid she'd chicken out if she called ahead, Amber took a chance he'd be home and went to Adam's apartment the next afternoon. Taking a deep breath when she stood before his door, she tried to quell the butterflies kickboxing in her stomach. She was doing what was right for her. She repeated the words like a mantra.

She knocked.

He opened the door a moment later and she almost forgot why she'd come. He looked wonderful. His shirt was unbuttoned, his sleeves rolled back over his arms, the cast still dominating one. His jeans were fitted, soft from wear and molding his long legs. His hair needed a trim but he still looked terrific. Her heart sped up.

"Amber, I didn't expect you," he said, opening the door wide. "Come in." Giving a hasty glance around the room, he evidently decided it was orderly enough for guests.

Like she cared. She hadn't come to see his apartment, she'd come to see him.

"I hope this is a good time," she said.

"Change your mind about going out tonight?" he asked as she walked nervously into the room. She twisted her fingers together, then purposefully pulled them apart. She raised her chin and turned to face him.

"No, I didn't change my mind about going out tonight. Actually, I thought it best if I came to tell you in person that I don't want us to see each other again."

He didn't move a muscle, just stared at her as the seconds ticked by.

"Mind telling me why?" he asked at last.

She studied him a moment, hoping she'd find the right words. He looked dark and intense and more fabulous than any man had a right to. She wasn't sure she had the courage to go through with this. But for her own sake, she had to. She did not want to be paralyzed with the pain of falling in love with someone only to lose them to an early death once more.

She wasn't brave enough for that.

"We're too different," she began.

"Most men and women are," he replied calmly. Only the clenched muscles in his cheeks gave the lie to that serenity. He was just able to cloak his tension. Amber wished she had that knack.

"Okay then. The real reason is that being with you scares me."

"I scare you?" Adam asked, astonished.

"Being with you does," she clarified. "There's a difference. Of course you don't scare me. You're kind and honorable and fun to be around. That's some of what scares me."

"I don't get it."

"I could fall for you," Amber blurted out. She refused to admit she already had. She would nip that infatuation in the bud. She was fighting to keep her heart whole and safe.

For the first time since she spoke, he seemed to relax.

"Well—"

"No, don't joke about it, Adam. I'm serious. I'm not up to that. Not now, maybe not ever. I don't want to fall in love. I don't want my life to be tied to someone else's. I don't want to be a hostage to fear the rest of my life."

"It's the firefighter thing, isn't it?"

"Partly. But only partly. I don't want to get caught up with anyone. It's safer."

"Safer than what?"

"Than being crushed when a person I love dies. I felt

that way in spring, before you met me. For several weeks, I didn't know if I could even get up in the morning."

"That's a natural progress of grieving. But you did get up, you moved ahead. I know it was tough losing Jimmy, but you got past it. You have your whole life ahead of you."

"And I'm feeling safe now. The worst of the grief is gone. But not all of it. And I remember. Now I have my baby to plan for, my schooling to finish and a job as a teacher to look forward to. I feel I'm in charge of things— and I like that. I want it to continue. I do not want to be at the whim of fate and risk losing someone close to me again. So I don't want to fall for you. I don't want to tempt fate by spending time with you and trying not to fall in love. It's better if we just end it now."

She wanted to dash from the apartment. She'd said what she'd come to say, now she needed to be alone.

But Adam didn't know that. And he had his own agenda.

"You don't mean that, Amber. You can't. We have something special going here. Something unexpected that neither one of us went looking for, but it found us anyway. I don't want to call it quits. I want to spend time with you, see if these feelings can grow and strengthen and give us each other."

She shook her head. She didn't want to hear anything like this. He had to agree to end things immediately. He had to!

"Hear me out," he said, stepping closer, placing his hands on her shoulders. She tried not to notice the tingling sensations his touch caused. She was hanging on by a thread.

"I've spent my entire adult life planning to play things safe, not get involved. I vowed never to be responsible for someone else. I wanted safe, too. But you changed that. Knowing you shows me what I'm missing."

"No. You're missing nothing. This is just sexual attraction, or forbidden fruit or something like that. You don't want a serious relationship," she said.

"I do. I want one with you. I love you, Amber."

She heard the words and panic flared once more.

Wrenching herself free, she turned as if cornered, seeking a way out. Adam blocked the path to the door.

"No, I don't want to hear this."

"Maybe you need to hear this, sweetheart. It changes everything. I love you. I want you to fall in love with me, for us to get married. We'll raise your baby and have others of our own. It's corny for a firefighter to say, but you light up my life. You set it on fire."

"No!" What if she fell for his line? What if she fell all the way in love with Adam, and he died? How could she bear the pain a second time? She couldn't do it.

"No. I don't want to see you again." She took a calming breath, tried to school her voice to betray none of the agitation she felt. This had not gone at all as she wished. She'd thought, hoped, he'd agree instantly.

For a moment, she was tempted. But she was not strong enough after all. She had to watch out for herself and her baby, and risking her heart again was not an option.

"I have to go, Adam. Please, respect my wishes. Don't call me, don't come by my apartment. Let's part as friends."

"I don't want to part," he said in frustration.

"Please, don't make this any harder than it is." Could she hold out? She felt like weakening when she looked into his eyes. She saw pain there. Was it reflected in her own?

"If it's hard, why do it?" he asked.

"I have to. I just have to."

He said nothing. After a moment, he stood aside and Amber almost ran to the door. In only seconds, she was on the sidewalk, heading toward the bus line. She didn't notice the once-familiar neighborhood. She only saw the pain in his eyes, and felt the pain in her heart.

She was doing the right thing. She knew she was. But it hurt.

"Better a short hurt now than after I really got to know him, made him part of my life. This will pass quickly. To go on would have threatened everything—my very existence," she told herself, hurrying as if to outrun her thoughts.

Adam heard the door open, but refused to look at her walking away. He couldn't believe it. He'd bared his soul, told her he'd loved her, asked her to marry him. And she'd said no.

Was this how Amber had felt when she heard Jimmy died? Was this what she feared? This emptiness? Feeling stunned, unable to accept facts? He wanted to run after her and make her listen. He loved her! He had never loved another woman. Had she heard him?

Of course she had. And it had been the last thing she wanted to hear. She'd come all the way to see him in person to tell him goodbye. She didn't want him to love her. She didn't want any commitment or ties.

If the truth be known, Adam wasn't sure he wanted to love her, either. Not now. Not when she'd spurned him without giving them a chance. But feelings had nothing much to do with wants.

Only guarantees might suit Amber, and those couldn't

be given. No one knew if he'd be alive tomorrow. He didn't want to cause her pain by dying young. But what if he lived to be eighty? She had thrown away his chance at happiness because of fear. Fear of something that might never happen.

Or could happen at the next fire, a voice in his head said.

If so, all the more reason to see each other as much as they could. Life was too short to ignore what was right in front of them. How could she throw it all away?

He threw himself down on the sofa, staring off into space. Life sucked. He'd been a fool to let down his guard and fall for a pretty blonde with an engaging smile. He wanted her with a power he hadn't known before. But she didn't want him. The irony wasn't lost on him. He'd fought love for so long—even the concept. Now he'd fallen right on his face. He should have never introduced himself all those weeks ago. God, he wanted her.

The next two weeks were the hardest in Amber's life. She missed Adam with an agonizing intensity that surprised her. The situation was made worse by the knowledge he loved her and she'd ended their relationship. And by the fact she could change it back if she'd just pick up the phone.

She was tempted. At night, when she was trying to sleep, she'd remember his words of love, his offer of marriage, and be so tempted to call him and say it was all a mistake.

But then she'd remember Jimmy. The searing pain of his loss had tempered over the months since his death. But she still felt overwhelmed some days. Afraid to face the feelings that had dominated for so long.

Then she'd think about Adam and their hours together, reliving every word, every gesture, every kiss. Rolling over, she'd try to sleep, but longing rose for another kiss. Just one. Or a walk with him holding her hand. The amusement that lurked in his eyes teased her in dreams. Yet they always ended with his walking away in disgust.

Awaking in the middle of the night almost became routine. Regrets flooded, yet the certainty of her stance kept her from calling him, from trying to see him again. Better this heartache now than heartbreak later.

Jill called to invite her to a cookout. Amber declined, saying she was busy getting ready for the next school year. If Jill thought it odd she couldn't take time out for an evening of fun, she didn't say anything. She did however, say, "You know Adam's been released from disability. He's back at work. I think he's doing a stint on the rescue squad temporarily, but I know he's glad to be back in the thick of things."

"I haven't spoken with him in a while. I'm glad he's okay." Amber clung to the phone, wishing she could ask more, find out if the arm healed without a problem. Was it his choice to be on the rescue squad, or did he want to be back on the front line? Did he ever mention her to his friends?

She would never know.

"Call me sometime and we'll go to lunch," Jill suggested.

Amber was tempted, but better to make the break clean. "I'll see, once I know my schedule." She wouldn't, of course, but no need to give a reason now. Jill would catch on when Amber never called.

"Okay then. Talk to you soon."

Hanging up the phone, Amber felt as if she'd severed the last tie. She should have felt better about things. But she didn't.

She burst into tears. She missed Adam so much she ached. It was as if he'd died, almost. Except she knew he was alive and doing what he loved. She would have to make do with that, and get on with her own life. She might not have the highs being with Adam gave, but at least she wouldn't be devastated if something happened to him.

On the second Wednesday in September, Amber and Virginia went to the hospital for the new parents orientation, which Amber had rescheduled, unable to face Virginia earlier. Sara and Matt had already taken their tour, so Amber didn't know anyone else in the small group. All the women were in late stages of pregnancy. One woman looked as if she was past due. Amber eyed her throughout the tour, wondering how big she'd get herself by the end.

"I had nothing like this," Virginia whispered when they saw the labor room. It was decorated like a bedroom, with chintz curtains and a rocking chair.

"Mom said it was totally different when she had me. She feels like this is the first baby for her since nothing's done the same." She wished she could be more interested, but nothing held her interest for long these days.

When they went to the nursery, they were able to look through the viewing window at babies lying in their plastic bassinets, wrapped in blue or pink blankets as was appropriate. In the far corner a woman rocked a baby. Two rocking chairs stood empty.

"This is where the babies are on display for family and friends. We have them here for a few hours a day, the rest of the time they are with the mother. And, of course, most are only here for a day or so, then we send them on their way home."

"Most but not all?" someone asked.

"If there are complications, we may keep them a little longer." She gestured to the woman rocking the baby. "We have volunteers who help when needed. Sometimes we have multiple births, or a mother has a problem that means she can't be with the baby, so our volunteers provide that important TLC. In fact, we always need more help, so if you have some spare time, join us."

A ripple of laughter passed through the group. None of the young mothers-to-be could foresee free time.

But Amber looked at Virginia. The older woman was staring at the babies, a sweet light in her eyes.

"You should volunteer," Amber said.

"Me? I don't know much about babies. I only had Jimmy. And he grew up so fast."

"You know how to rock them, hold them. Think about it. You have time and this is a need that would be fun to fulfill."

Virginia looked thoughtful. "I'll have my hands full with my granddaughter," she said slowly.

"No, you won't. You can come to visit and she'll visit you, but Virginia, this is not your child. You need something to do in life that will give you more purpose than planning to spoil my daughter. Think about it," Amber said firmly. She was taking charge of her life with a vengeance, she thought. But she was adamant about not letting Virginia take over a major facet of her baby's life.

"Maybe I will think about it," Virginia said, looking at the babies again.

Virginia drove Amber back to her apartment when the tour was over.

"Are you still seeing that man?" she asked on the drive.

"If you mean Adam, no, I haven't seen him since the day after he kindly assembled my baby's bedroom furniture."

Virginia was silent for a moment. "I'm thinking about packing up Jimmy's room," she said slowly. "James thinks we should make it into a guest room where you and the baby can come to stay from time to time. I know we live close, but maybe you'll want us to watch the baby in the evening or something when you go out, and then just stay over rather than waken her."

"Are you sure?" Amber asked. She could hear the sadness in her voice.

"I'm not throwing things away. Some of his things we'll keep on display. But most of it has no meaning except to Jimmy and to me. I'll pack the boxes away. Maybe the baby will like to see them when she's older."

"Of course she would. And we have to make sure she knows all about her father. How good he was in sports, how much he loved to pig out on popcorn, and how much he loved all of us."

"It's so hard, Amber. I hope you die long before your baby does," Virginia said.

Amber covered the older woman's hand as it held the steering wheel. "I want to name her Jamie Marie, for Jimmy."

Virginia smiled. "A lovely name."

They drove in silence until Virginia pulled to a stop in front of Amber's apartment building. "That man was right, you know. One day you will fall in love again and marry. Just don't let Jamie Marie forget her grandparents."

"Virginia, if I ever marry again, that won't change Jamie's grandparents. She'll spend lots of time with you two, no matter what. I'm counting on that. I never knew any of my grandparents. I would never deprive my child of the opportunity to know and love hers."

"Your new husband might object to that," she said.

"Then he wouldn't be the kind of man I'd want to marry in the first place. But I have no plans to marry, so there's no need to worry."

"What about Adam?"

"We aren't seeing each other anymore," Amber said. "If I ever fall in love again, I want someone in a safe job, not to risk losing him because of what he does."

"When you're ready, I'll have James introduce you to some nice safe insurance salesmen," Virginia said.

Amber laughed. "That's a deal."

Would she ever be ready for anyone else after Adam?

"I think you're nuts," Bets said as she and Amber walked across the campus. The fall day was sunny, with a breeze from the west keeping the temperatures comfortable. The campus was full of students sauntering from building to building, checking out their schedules and arranging meetings with friends.

"You've said that every time we've talked lately," Amber said. "Your opinion is duly noted."

"But ignored," her friend said cheerfully.

"What else can I do?"

"Nothing. If you've gone three weeks and don't miss him, you were right, he's not for you."

"I miss him," she said slowly. "But it's too soon to think about getting involved with anyone. Maybe I'll feel differently in a while. But right now the fear of loss is huge. You don't get it. No one could who hasn't experienced a sudden loss like I did. I live with it every day. What if something happens to my mother? Or to Matt. He jets all over the world. What if the plane crashes?"

"Hey, flying's safer than driving. Statistically speaking, more people live to old age than die young, thought of that?"

"Not in the Army."

"Yep, even there. Or firefighters. Or cops, or wild animal trainers."

"Wild animal trainers?" Amber said.

"Well, it's another dangerous profession."

Amber laughed. "I'll keep that in mind if I ever run into one. Let's change the subject."

"To?"

"Do you think we'll like Dr. Scrubs?"

"Not a bit. A pompous ass, if you ask me. But he's the only one teaching that course this semester, so we're stuck. Gives us a good opportunity to learn to deal with problem parents. We'll practice on him. And your mother-in-law."

"She's getting better." Amber defended her.

"Impossible."

"Really, she is. She started working at the hospital as a volunteer in the newborn section and loves it. She goes there every day now to rock the babies and help the nurses however she can. It's her new hobby."

"You said she needed one."

They reached the intersection on busy 19th Avenue. Amber was heading for her bus stop across the street, while Bets would be returning to the library to look up some facts for a paper she wanted to start. For a moment Amber felt a pang she wasn't returning to the apartment she'd had— in the building with Adam's apartment. If she hadn't moved, she would have run into him by now. Even though she knew she wasn't strong enough to stand up to a committed relationship between them, she would have been able to catch a glimpse of him from time to time.

Would that have been better or worse?

Bets waited with her at the traffic light. "I'll call you later and let you know if that topic will work."

"You can make it work," Amber said. "I haven't a clue what I want to write about for my term project. Hopefully something will come to me soon."

When the light changed she said a quick goodbye.

"I'll call you," Bets said as Amber began to cross the wide street.

Out of nowhere a car sped toward the crosswalk, running the red light. Amber turned at Bets' cry, and saw the driver's horrified face, heard the screech of brakes. Events seemed to move in slow motion. Before she could react, the edge of the bumper caught her and spun her around, knocking her off her feet. Instinctively she dropped her books to cradle her baby, rolling into a ball as she fell. She felt as if she were swimming through cold molasses. The sounds vied with one another: Bets screaming her name, the sound of cars jolting to a stop, a horn blowing somewhere. Confusion reigned.

Until she cracked her head on the pavement and everything went black.

CHAPTER ELEVEN

"AMBER? Wake up. Come on, you can do it. Amber, it's Adam. Wake up."

Slowly the words began to make sense. Amber opened her eyes, shutting them tightly at the brightness which hurt her head.

"*Ohhh,*" she moaned. Pain seemed to explode everywhere.

"That's it, open your eyes. You're going to be all right."

Adam's strong voice continued to urge her to wake up, but she didn't want to. Her head throbbed. Her hip ached.

"What happened? Where am I?" she asked.

Memory clicked. "Oh, no. Is the baby okay? Adam!" She opened her eyes and reached for his arm, clutching it tightly. "Adam, is my baby okay?"

"We're transporting you to the hospital as soon as possible. Stay with me. You're going to be fine. We're taking you in as soon as the ambulance gets here."

He put a stethoscope on and pumped up an arm cuff already wrapped around her arm, listening for her blood pressure readings. He called a number to someone to her left.

Amber looked over at another E.M.T. jotting notes on a clipboard.

"ETA for the ambulance is two minutes," he murmured, glancing at Amber and smiling. "You're in good hands, miss. Adam and I are the best."

"Modest, too," Adam murmured. "We're putting you on a backboard, to hold your head and neck immobile. Just a precaution. Where else hurts?"

"My hip. My head is killing me. What happened?"

"Car ran the red light. Clipped you on the hip. Damn driver was drunk. It's only eleven-thirty in the morning, for Pete's sake."

Amber felt fuzzy. She closed her eyes. "It's so bright. Are you sure Jamie is okay?"

"Who's Jamie?" Adam asked, glancing around. There had only been the one victim.

"She's named the baby Jamie," Bets said.

Amber opened her eyes and looked around. "Bets?"

"Right here." Her hand came out to pat Amber gently on the shoulder. "God, you scared me to death. I thought you were a goner until these guys showed up. Isn't this a kick? Adam is working the paramedic shift today and he was the first response."

"How is she?" an unfamiliar voice asked.

Amber squinted up at a uniformed police officer. Too many people, too much confusion. She closed her eyes, willing the pain to subside.

"We'll have her in the hospital for a complete workup, but I think she'll make it," Adam said. "You can check with the doctor later to arrange for questioning."

"Don't think we need to bother her. Plenty of witnesses," the policeman said, tapping his notebook. "And we have the driver."

"Am I losing you, Amber?" Adam asked.

"I'm sleepy."

"Wait a little longer."

In only a short time, Amber was strapped to a back-board, a cervical collar in place and she felt herself being lifted into the cool dimness of the ambulance. She reached out and grabbed Adam.

"Come with me," she said. She'd just been thinking about catching a glimpse of him. Now he was here. And doing his job. He hadn't once looked at her with the old friendliness, or that amusement in his eyes.

Were her injuries serious, or had he closed down because of her last declaration?

She was so glad to see him, despite the circumstances.

"We'll be right behind you," Adam said.

"Please, can't you ride with me? I'm scared." Not of the hospital, not of her injuries, though they could be serious. Amber was afraid of the gladness that swept through her being near Adam. She'd missed him so much, as if a part of her had been cut out and was now restored.

A moment's discussion and Adam climbed into the ambulance. The vehicle pulled away from the scene and gained speed.

Amber was vaguely aware of the siren, but her focus was on Adam. He sat beside her, one hand holding her wrist, his face impassive as he noted her vital stats.

"I didn't expect to see you again," she murmured, wanting some attention. The ambulance attendant sat on the other side of the stretcher, monitoring the oxygen she was getting.

"It scared me to death," Adam said, "when we got there and I saw you were the one on the ground."

"I'm really going to be all right?"

"I think so. And no problems with the baby as far as I can tell. The doctor will let you know for certain. You sheltered her as you fell. Instinctively. Mothers do that."

"It happened so fast."

"They caught the man. He rammed his car into a parked one and just sat there."

"Is he okay?"

"Drunk as a skunk. Too limber from booze to sustain serious injury," Adam said with disgust. "The police took him into custody."

"I could have been killed," Amber said slowly. "In just a heartbeat. One minute I was talking to Bets, the next I was crossing the street and that man could have killed me and my baby."

"But he didn't. Don't dwell on it. Focus on getting better as fast as you can."

Adam watched her close her eyes. There was a bruise on her forehead where she'd hit the pavement. The preliminary examination at the site hadn't indicated any broken bones, but she needed X-rays to confirm that.

There was plenty of bruising, especially on her hip at the point of impact where the car had grazed her. Serious enough; however, had she been a couple of feet farther into the crosswalk, the car would have hit her square in the middle, probably tossing her into the air, with an outcome likely far different from what they had.

He wanted to beat the hell out of that driver. How dare he endanger others with his drunken behavior? He hoped the judge threw the book at him.

He'd never forget the fear that struck when he'd climbed out of the rescue truck and recognized Amber. For a split second, he'd thought her dead. Then his training kicked in and he and Greg had got to work.

She was going to be fine, he reassured himself, willing the helplessness to fade. He'd done his job and she was going to walk out of the hospital on her own two feet. Her hand was scraped. Lightly he rubbed his thumb on the unabraded skin next to the scrape. It was so soft. He hated to think of the trauma her body had gone through. He just hoped the baby was safe. He knew it took a lot to dislodge a healthy fetus. And Amber couldn't lose her baby after losing her husband. Adam couldn't bear the thought of that.

She might not want him in her life, but he wanted her in his. Wished things had been so different. But he respected her too much to push in where he wasn't wanted. He'd given it his best shot and she'd said no. End of discussion.

Amber had slipped back into unconsciousness by the time they reached the hospital. Adam gave the E.R. doctor a quick report, then watched as Amber was wheeled into an examination cubicle.

He went to find a phone. He looked up Matt's office phone number and called the man. Better he tell Sara than Adam.

Then he called Virginia Woodworth.

Adam was filling out the incident report when Bets hurried into the Emergency Room. "Is she okay?" she asked, coming over to him when she recognized a familiar face.

"Doctor's still with her. I've called her stepfather and mother-in-law. They're on their way here. Can you stay in case she needs someone before they come?"

"I can. You won't?" Bets asked.

"I'm on duty. As soon as I finish the accident report, I'll be back in service and may have to respond to another call. Besides, she doesn't want me here." He studied the report, pleased to note his voice had masked the pain he felt at the words.

"Don't be too sure of that. She cares for you a lot more than she wants to admit," Bets said. "Don't write her off just yet."

"She has a funny way of showing it," he commented, jotting down the final comments. For a moment he wanted to let hope in, but Amber had been brutally frank refusing his offer of marriage and spurning his declaration of love. Adam had too much pride to push in where he wasn't wanted.

"She's just scared of being hurt again," Bets said.

"There are all kinds of hurts. Did she tell you I asked her to marry me and she said no? What does she think turning me down did to me?" he asked, then could have kicked himself. He didn't need to parade the hurt Amber had inflicted. He'd get over it.

"She's not thinking, she's reacting. Give her another chance," Bets pleaded.

"If she asks, tell her I'll stop back later, when we get a dinner break. I'm on duty until tomorrow morning. But I'll check in to see how she's doing." He jotted his cell phone number on a slip of paper and gave it to Bets, asking her to call him as soon as she knew how Amber was doing. Amber never had to know he'd asked after her. If she didn't want to see him, he wouldn't intrude when he stopped back by.

He couldn't get over the clutch of fear that had grasped him when he saw her lying motionless on the pavement. Of course he'd check in. He needed to know she was really going to be fine. He wished he could stay, but duty called. Reassuring himself she was in good hands, he went back to the rescue truck, which Greg had already restocked.

"Ready to roll?" Greg asked.

"As ready as I'll ever be," Adam replied, wishing he could stay with Amber. For the first time ever, he resented his job and the need to be away when he longed to stay.

It was shortly after seven when Adam returned to the hospital and located the floor where Amber was. He was on his dinner break and had had Greg drop him off.

Bets had called several hours ago to say everything looked okay with Amber, except for bruising and a slight concussion. They were holding her overnight to monitor the baby and the concussion. By the time Bets called, both Amber's parents and the Woodworths had arrived. He felt better knowing she had her family with her, people she cared about and who loved her.

He arrived at the open door to her room, feeling awkward and uncertain. Maybe he'd just peep in and make sure she was all right. She didn't want to see him.

Amber lay in bed, propped up and talking with her mother. Sara sat beside the bed, lines of worry etched around her eyes. Matt sat beside her, rubbing her back as if in support.

"Adam!" Amber caught sight of him and her entire face lit up.

"Hey," he said.

Amber smiled. "Bets said you'd be back later. Come in."

Sara rose and went to greet Adam, giving him a hard hug. "Thank you for taking such good care of her," she said. "I was scared to death when Matt came home to get me. But I figured she was in the best hands possible until I could get here."

Matt followed, offering his hand, gripping Adam's firmly. "I want to thank you, too. She's kind of special, you know?"

Adam nodded, looking at Amber again. How very special these people would never know.

"Just doing my job," he said.

"Then thank you for taking on such a job."

Sara looked at Amber and back at Adam. "If you can stay a few minutes, I need to take a walk. We'll be back soon, sweetie," Sara said to Amber. Then she looked at her husband. In only seconds they disappeared down the hallway.

"Smooth move, Mom," Amber said, wryly.

"How are you doing?" Adam asked, going to sit on the chair Sara had vacated.

"My head is throbbing like bongo drums, but they don't want to give me any medication because of the concussion. My hip hurts if I move an inch, or if the baby kicks and stretches the skin. My hands ache, my shoulder aches and I hope I never take perfect health for granted again."

"But you're fine, other than that?"

She nodded. "I'll be various shades of purple and green for a month, I'm sure, but the doctor said I'll be fine. And the baby is fine. I'm staying overnight just as a precaution."

She held out her hand. Adam looked at it for a long moment, then reached out and gently took it in his. Her skin was warm and soft. He rubbed his thumb over the smooth texture. He'd come so close to losing her. Even if he never saw her again, he wanted her to live a long happy life.

Amber looked at him greedily, taking in the crisp uniform he wore, his dark hair, the tiredness around his eyes. She hadn't seen him in weeks. He wasn't staying long, so she had to feast her eyes on him until he left.

"Adam, I wanted to talk to you. I told my mother, that's

why she and Matt disappeared so fast. I could have been killed today."

He looked at her and shook his head. "Don't think about that. You're going to be fine."

"I know that. And I'm so grateful. But I could have been killed. If I'd been a couple of feet farther into the intersection, or if that driver had swerved more to the left, I would be dead."

"Amber—"

"No, let me finish. It made me think. Here I am, a college student. How innocuous can you get? My most dangerous thing should be if I drop a textbook on my foot. And yet I was almost killed."

"But you weren't. Don't think that way, honey. You're going to be fine." He didn't want to think another second about what might have been. For the first time he had a glimmer of understanding of Amber's position. It would hurt like hell to hear of her death. No wonder she didn't want to risk another relationship.

"This is important, Adam. I could have been killed and I don't have a dangerous job. I was just crossing the street. I've been so worried that I'd fall for a guy with a dangerous profession—but I'm the one who was almost killed. It's made me think. I've talked about this with Bets and my mother. If I had died today do you know what I would have regretted the most?"

Adam shook his head, his gaze locked with hers. He knew what he would regret.

"That I hadn't given us a chance. I've been so busy trying to protect myself, I haven't been looking at things clearly. Bets told me that. So did my mother. I'm responsible for my actions, and for the way I live my life. I don't want to become a woman afraid of shadows, afraid of things that may never happen. Jimmy didn't get to live out a full life with me. In a way, I need to be living for Jimmy as well. Doing all the things he would have loved. Making sure his daughter has the best life possible, and that the girl Jimmy loved remembers him always and lives life to the fullest as he would have done. He sure as certain would never hole up and wall off anything that would give him excitement and adventure and happiness."

"You need a chance to heal from his loss," Adam said.

"I do. And I am healing. But I'm not going to eliminate risk from my life because I might get hurt. The flipside of everything bad is everything good. What if I had died today? You would feel sad. But you'd go on. I feel sad Jimmy died, but I need to go on. He was wiser than me, he even told me to move on with life. So for Jimmy, and for me, I want the best life has to offer."

Adam nodded. He wanted the best life had to offer for her as well. He just wished he was part of it.

He squeezed her hand and stood. "I have to go." She didn't need to know that he still had plenty of time on his break. He couldn't stay here and listen to her and not take her into his arms. He wanted to demand she allow him to be a part of her life, and that she be a part of his.

"Not yet," she protested, her hand clutching his. "Stay, please. Stay in my life forever."

From the stunned look on Adam's face, Amber knew her words weren't what he'd been expecting. Maybe not even what he wanted to hear. Had he had time to reconsider? Had the words of love been foolishly said, later regretted?

"In your life as in?" he asked, as if for clarification.

"However you see me in it." She almost held her breath. Why didn't he sweep her into his arms? Was she too late? Had he changed his mind? Or had he not loved her at all.

Maybe he needed to know how she felt.

"I love you, Adam. I'm sorry I was hurtful last time we met. I was scared. I'm still scared. But now I'm more afraid of messing up the best thing in my life by being fearful of the unknown."

"A sudden change," he said. "See how you feel in a couple of days. You're emotional because of the accident."

"I know my mind. I've known it for a while, though I've tried to fight against it. How do you see me in your life, Adam?"

"I don't."

She felt as if he'd just jerked the bed out from under her. "You don't?"

"You made it clear the other day you don't want me in yours. Today changed nothing really, did it? Wait until you recover, until the concussion heals, until you're on your feet again, then see how you feel."

"I don't need to wait, Adam. I know how I feel."

"A bump on the head changes nothing."

"No. I loved you before. I was afraid to admit it—to me or to you. And I'm still afraid, but even more so of not sharing whatever time we are allotted together. Please, Adam, don't tell me I'm too late."

He didn't say anything. Amber's heart fell.

"Please," she whispered. Had his love been so ephemeral it had already vanished?

"You asked me how I see you in my life. If I had my way, I'd see you as my wife," he said slowly. "That hasn't changed."

"Oh wow." Amber burst into tears. "You meant it before? You do love me?"

"Of course I meant it before, what did you think?" Adam said, reaching up to brush the tears from her cheeks.

"That it sounded like a proposal which I foolishly turned down," she said, sniffing. "I want a do-over. I want to accept."

He stared at her. "You'll marry me?"

She nodded, tightening the grip she had on his hand. "I love you, Adam. It's not emotions from the accident, not delusions from the concussion. It's real, and important, and strong. I've fought hard, thought I was doing the right thing. But I've been so miserable without you. I love you."

He reached out to gather her up in a gentle hug. "Oh, sweetheart, not half as much as I love you." Then he kissed her.

The blood pounding made her headache even worse, like hammers over every inch. But Amber didn't care. Adam loved her! He wanted to marry her. Together they'd share a lifetime of ups and downs and happiness. For however long their life together was to be.

Endless moments later, they pulled apart, looking into each other's eyes.

"I'm so happy I could dance," Amber said. She frowned and put her free hand to her forehead. "Except my head hurts so much I can hardly stand it."

"You should feel better by morning. How soon will you marry me?" Adam said.

"I rushed through my wedding for Jimmy. He only had a few weeks' stateside duty. I want this to be special. Not a big wedding, but not a rushed one. Is that okay?"

"Take your time, sweetheart. When it's time, we'll do it."

"Don't think I'm stalling, I just don't want to rush. But

I can't wait to become your wife. We should get married before Jamie Marie shows up, don't you think? You won't mind having a ready-made, instant family, will you?"

"Once I get used to it, I'm going to be on top of the world. But five minutes ago I thought I wouldn't see you again, and now—"

"Of course you also get my mother and Matt, and the Woodworths as well. They'll always be Jamie's grandparents."

"No problem. I don't have any parents. They can be grandparents to all our kids if you like," Adam said, drawing her into his arms.

"All our kids?" Amber repeated.

"You didn't want to stop at one, did you?"

"I hadn't thought about it, but no, I don't want only one. Mostly I was thinking I hoped I got a chance to tell you I was wrong. Bets said she thought I was nuts. Even my mother questioned what I'd been thinking about. I'm sorry I got hurt, but maybe it is a blessing in disguise. How long would it have taken me to come to my senses if I hadn't?"

He shook his head, "I haven't a clue. Let's not think about what might have been, but about what is. Marry me and let's grow old together."

EPILOGUE

November 22

"THE line is still busy," Matt said in disgust.

Sara started to say something but the pain gripped her so tightly she could hardly breathe. She held still, holding her swollen belly, riding through the contraction.

Matt went to hold her. "Breathe, darling. Remember the Lamaze classes. Panting breaths will help you through it. We can't wait any longer. We've told the doctor we're on our way to the hospital. We'll call from there."

"She must be talking to Bets. There will still be time for her to get to the hospital for the baby's birth if we keep trying. I just wanted her there from the beginning."

"I know. Let me call Dex. He can keep trying. That way we can concentrate on getting you to the hospital and not worry about a thing."

Sara smiled. "Okay, Daddy. Let's do it."

"Try one more time," Amber said.

"We need to leave, not keep calling when they're obviously on the line or something. Every time I've called for the last half hour, the line has been busy," Adam said.

"Well, try one more time."

"Once more, then we leave. I do *not* plan to deliver our little girl. That's what they have doctors for."

"You'd do a great job," Amber said. "Oh. This hurts! I never knew it would be so painful. *Darndarndarndarn-darn.*"

Adam took one of her hands and brought it to his mouth where he kissed it, squeezing hard as if trying to divert her attention from the labor pains to the ache in her hand. He hit redial on the phone.

"It's ringing."

Amber leaned back against the sofa, already gearing up for the next contraction. She should have let Adam call earlier, when the contractions first started. But she knew first babies could take a long time and there was no need for everyone to be in an uproar if the birth was hours away.

"No answer," he said when he heard the answering machine click on.

"Matt, Sara, it's Adam. Amber is in labor. We're heading for the hospital now. See you there."

He tossed the phone on the sofa. "Now, let's go."

"Maybe we should try the doctor again," Amber said.

"We left a message with his service, who guaranteed to locate him. He'll beat us there. And—"

"I know, you don't want to deliver this baby!"

The nurse met Sara and Matt at the door with a wheelchair. "Sit down, dear, you'll feel better," she said.

Sara sat down, still clinging to Matt's hand. "The contractions are coming so close together. I don't remember going this fast with Amber."

"Second babies often come quickly," the nurse said as

she pushed her smoothly along the corridor to the elevator. In only moments they were whisked to the fourth floor, labor and delivery.

"Is Dr. Anderson here yet?" Matt asked.

"He is. And a busy man, too. Another of his patients is on the way as well. Here we go. Now, here's your gown. Shall your husband help you?" the nurse asked, shaking out the shortie nightgown the hospital used for deliveries. It pulled over the head, with the back completely intact.

"Yes," Sara said, then groaned as another contraction hit.

"Timing," the nurse said, glancing at her watch.

The room was decorated as a bedroom in a private home might have been. The wallpaper was light and cheery, the furnishings of polished oak. There were frilly curtains on the windows. A comfortable chair and a rocking chair sat along the wall. Only the high hospital bed gave any indication this wasn't someone's favorite bedroom.

But Sara wasn't interested in the decor. She was fighting to stay on top of the pain.

By the time she'd gotten dressed, with Matt's help, she'd had two more contractions.

"This baby is anxious to be born," the nurse said, helping Sara into bed. "I'll pop out and let the doctor know."

Matt stepped behind her, rubbing her back, one hand on her belly.

"Hang in there, sweetheart. I'm with you every step of the way."

"Wish we could trade places," she grumbled.

"Dr. Anderson is a busy man. He has another patient already checked in," the young nurse said as she helped Amber change into a hospital issue gown.

"Sara Tucker?" Adam hazarded a guess.

"That's right, how did you know?"

He laughed. "This is one for the books. Sara is Amber's mother."

The nurse looked at Amber, then Adam. "Her mother? But she's delivering a baby."

Amber nodded, then began panting. Adam stepped up to support her. "Focus, Amber. Remember what we learned."

It wasn't often a honeymoon was spent in Lamaze classes rather than on the beach in some resort, but that's the way Adam and Amber spent their first few weeks of marriage.

None of the family had offered even a token resistance to the union after Amber's brush with death. Even Virginia Woodworth had given her blessing. Their real honeymoon would be taken later, when finals were over and Amber was recovered from the birth of Jamie Marie.

Now the birth was imminent, and she couldn't wait to hold her baby girl in her arms.

"Breathe, honey," Adam instructed.

"I am breathing. You try this for a while. Ow-ow-ow-ow, darn it, this hurts! Go find Mom and tell her I'm here."

"I can't leave you," Adam said calmly. "We'll get the nurse to let her know." He turned to the young woman and asked if she would relay a message to Sara Tucker. She assured him she would, as soon as she notified the doctor how close Amber was to delivery.

"Go find Amber. Tell her I'm here," Sara said.

"The nurse told us she knows you're here. And I'm not leaving you. Let her own husband take care of her."

Dr. Anderson came in, wearing scrubs. "So, we're about to have a baby, are we?"

"And Amber," Sara said, clinging to Matt's hand.

"And Amber. I've sent my resident to check on her. If you deliver fast enough, I can get over there for that one as well. She's two doors down." The doctor sat on a rolling stool and moved into position.

"Crowning already. You are in a hurry, Mrs. Tucker."

"Not. Getting. Any. Younger," Sara said through breaths. She gripped Matt's hand tightly and tried to smile up at him. "You better appreciate this baby," she said.

"Darling, I appreciate you and our baby." He kissed her gently, the kiss interrupted as another contraction tore through her.

"Do you know what to do?" Adam asked the resident as he checked Amber.

"If not, my husband can deliver the baby. He's an E.M.T.," Amber said, unsure as Adam about the experience of the young man at the foot of the high bed.

"I've delivered several babies in the last month alone," the resident said. "You'll be fine, I guarantee it."

Amber looked at Adam. "Stand ready to move in if I need you," she said softly.

"I heard that," the doctor said, smiling at her. "I'd say you're going to be a mother very soon."

"Two-fifteen exactly," Dr. Anderson said as he glanced at the clock once he held the baby boy in his hands. He placed him gently on Sara's stomach and prepared for the afterbirth.

"Oh, he's so darling," she cooed.

Matt studied him. "Not as big as I thought he'd be. And he needs a bath."

She giggled. "He's beautiful. And he'll grow up big and strong like his daddy."

"I love you, Sara," he said, leaning over to kiss her.

"Two-fifteen exactly," the resident said, as he handed the baby girl to Adam. "Here, Papa, hold your daughter."

Adam took the baby in the blanket the nurse gave him as the resident clipped the cord. He brought her to where Amber could see her. "Our daughter," he said proudly.

"She's so tiny. But perfect, isn't she?" Amber said, touching her gently, counting her fingers and toes.

"She's as perfect as her mother," Adam said, leaning over to kiss her. "Wouldn't her father be proud!"

"As proud as her daddy is already," Amber said. "I love you, Adam."

"And I love you, Mrs. Carruthers. Now and for always."

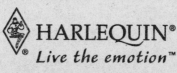

If you enjoyed what you just read,
then we've got an offer you can't resist!

Take 2 bestselling love stories FREE!

Plus get a FREE surprise gift!

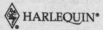